CHAPTER ONE

'Now tell me. Why the secrecy?' Vido's PA demanded. 'Why was I forbidden to mention your name during the purchase of this house? And why did you want it so badly that you paid over the odds?'

More than a little petulant, Camilla Lycett-Brown swung her long legs into his car and tried to make sense of the extraordinary tension that ran through Vido's entire body.

Injustice! he wanted to snarl, with a bitterness that startled him. But he realised how powerfully his Italian blood burned in his veins, despite having an English father—whoever he was—and living in England for the first eighteen years of his life.

At that age he'd fled to Italy with his mother and ever since, the scouring injustice had clawed and chewed and nagged at him. Slowly and viciously it had taken over his life till he knew he had to take steps to seek a solution of his own—or lose his sanity.

'My late mother worked here,' he said abruptly. 'As a cook.'

The memories of that time flooded back, tearing at him cruelly. The insults. The humiliation and betrayal.

His jaw tight, he took one last look at the historic Elizabethan building in the small village of Shottery. He had owned Stanford House for the past two weeks but this had been his first visit since it had been purchased from the bankrupt George Willoughby.

For you, Mama, he said in silent offering. One of his goals achieved. Two more to come and then he could rest easy.

'And?' Camilla was astute enough to know there was more to it than he was saying.

Wondering how much to tell her, he drove away, towards the elaborate wrought-iron gates. But when they hummed smoothly shut behind the car, he found his hands shaking so much that he had to switch off the ignition.

Turning his head, he glowered back at the house. The early-April sunshine illuminated the stately façade with a welcoming warmth. This belonged to him now! A sudden explosion of excitement made it hard for him to breathe. Such a building, such a lifestyle, had once seemed utterly beyond his reach.

Acquiring Stanford meant more to him than turning around the family business in Italy and putting it into profit. More, too, than his formidable reputation in Milan as the only conceivable man to call in whenever a company teetered on the brink of extinction.

Because this little triumph was deeply personal.

'Mother was sacked. Unfairly.'

His voice was quiet, his eyes hard and unforgiving. The specialist had confided that his beloved mother's ME had initially been triggered by the stress of Willoughby's impossible demands. It saddened Vido that she had died before she could enjoy the luxuries he could provide. He mourned her deeply and would fulfil his vow to her, whatever it took.

'That started off a chain of events that soured her life and mine.' His eyes narrowed. 'We went through hell. I was still at school but I took night-shift work in a factory owned by the same man who lived in Stanford House.' He hesitated. What the hell. It might help to confide in her. 'Then he threw me out of the factory for theft—even though he *knew* his daughter had framed me. They caused me to be vilified as a *thief*!'

He spat out the word, still incapable of containing his horror at the sickening shame he'd felt. The proud lines of his face were riven with a grim anger and Camilla cringed back in her seat, suddenly afraid of this unknown, dark side to Vido's nature.

'I intend,' he continued grimly, 'to make them apologise for what they did. I promised my mother I would clear our name. I need closure on Willoughby and his shrew of a daughter. That's all you need to know.'

'This…isn't like you,' Camilla ventured uncertainly.

'You don't know the humiliation they put me through. It was like a physical pain to be treated like a leper. The people I'd worked with spat at me.' He took a moment to get himself together. This was screwing him up, big time. 'The daughter was clever. She made sure that the stolen money came from a fund that the workers had saved for a works outing.'

'So how did the daughter frame you?' Camilla asked, round-eyed.

'She planted the cash in my locker.'

'Why would she do that?' His PA's cut-glass accent was more pronounced than ever.

There was a tightening of his jaw. 'Spite. We'd had a row. She accused me of sleeping around while I was dating her. And of planning to marry her for her inheritance.' His eyes gleamed and his mouth was savage.

'I imagine you weren't.'

He gave her a filthy look. 'I was so shocked I could hardly speak. Now do you understand how passionate I feel about this?'

'Oh, yes. Was she beautiful?' Camilla asked a little shakily.

With a jerk of rogue emotion in his chest he recalled the sixteen-year-old Anna; long-legged and lissom with a sexuality that had given him dreams at night. And of her nose that had been so large and deformed that she'd been called a witch from nursery school onwards.

He shrugged. 'I loved her. God knows why. She'd seemed sweet and innocent and made me laugh. But underneath she was a heartless little bitch.'

The more he thought of Anna's malice, the angrier he became. But she'd get her come-uppance too. He didn't know where she was, but he'd find her. And make her life a living nightmare till he had what he wanted.

His eyes gleamed like pan-warmed chocolate beneath the arrowed arches of his fair brows. It was ironic that Willoughby had lost both his fortune and Stanford House. Whilst he, the illegitimate son of the old man's cook, was no longer dirt poor and starving, but rich beyond his wildest childhood dreams—and still two years short of thirty.

He gave a sardonic laugh, his head tipping back and catching the sun that glinted on his flowing hair, turning it to a rich pale gold. His teeth shone pearly in an olive skin that had been deepened to a dark honey shade from ten years of Italian sunshine.

A little curl of desire rippled through Camilla's shapely body because Vido was breathtakingly beautiful. Her elegant hand turned his chin. Her lips were on his before he could draw away and he suffered the kiss in silence, even making a half-hearted attempt at deepening the embrace.

So his appetite for women was still subnormal. He fumed in frustration. Anna's fault. She'd all but castrated him where love was concerned. His wounded heart had hardened and no woman had melted even a little corner in all his years in Italy.

He wanted to love Camilla and had tried his very best to do so. She was a brilliant hostess, witty and clever and an asset to his business. He longed for a wife and children. But these— and peace of mind—were unattainable unless he felt he had dealt with his demons in his own, inimitable way.

'Let's go,' he said huskily and felt guilty when Camilla looked pleased, perhaps assuming his choking emotion was due to a different passion.

Dark eyes stone-cold with ruthless intent, he started up the car and swung out into Cottage Lane, heading for his office in London.

Anna knelt on the garden path, her capable fingers busily tweaking out weeds from the colourful herbaceous borders of the typically English cottage garden.

Sitting back to review the results of her labours, she couldn't help but be struck by the contrast with the magnificent gardens of Stanford House, where she'd once lived. This little patch in the front garden was all she had now. Ten feet by six. A far cry from the acres where she'd once roamed, a lonely, unloved—and unlovely—girl.

Almost unthinkingly, her muddy fingers went to her nose. Now it was a normal size and fitted her face properly. She smiled with gentle pleasure.

But being ugly had left her a lasting legacy. She was even more careful not to reveal her feelings to anyone. The episode with Vido had cured her of that.

Anna frowned and tackled a stubborn dock root with grim determination, pushing back the pain that had leapt to squeeze her heart like a vice. Why open old wounds? Sure she'd loved him, madly, wildly, deeply, although she hadn't dared say so in case he'd laughed at her temerity. After all, he'd been the most popular boy in school and she'd been—what had those girls said?—*a hideous little bat.*

OK, he'd kissed her several times, and she'd hardly been able to believe her luck. But her grandfather and the girls at school had told her why he was dating her. He was ambitious as hell and she was an heiress. Why else would an Adonis suck up to someone as hideous as her?

She bit her lip, suffering once again the hard nails of painful truth. Her world had come crashing about her ears that day when she'd been forced to accept that Vido was just a callous fortune-hunter. She'd been a means to an end. Nothing more.

Anna frowned. He was yesterday's news. Soon she'd be married and she'd be able to forget her hurt and the lack of self-esteem that still haunted her.

Thankfully, her fiancé, Peter, liked her silences and her quiet reserve. He hated emotional, demonstrative women. And she was lucky to have found someone who appreciated her qualities. A matter-of-fact and rather cool man, who was very attentive but didn't arouse horrible, uncontrollable longings that scared her with their raw intensity.

A screech of brakes came from the lane and then the sound of a reversing car, but she paid no attention. When Stanford House had been sold, precipitating her grandfather's stroke, she'd taken over the nearby cottage that in better times had belonged to their gardener.

It was situated only two hundred yards from the beautiful old farmhouse where Shakespeare's wife, Anne Hathaway, had been born. Passing tourists often stopped to admire and photograph her tiny black and white timbered cottage with its picturesque thatched roof, too.

Wistfully she mused that it would be nice if her grandfather could appreciate the cottage's charm. But it was unlikely. He had railed against his bankruptcy and hated what he called 'coming down in the world'.

It wasn't surprising that he'd had a stroke. Her heart went out to him. He'd changed from being a gruff and domineering man and now looked helpless and frightened. She decided to pick him some flowers. Hopefully there would be better news about him when she next visited.

Tensely Vido glowered at the woman's slender back and the mass of gleaming black hair. Even after ten years, Anna's spectacular body was unmistakable. So were his conflicting emotions.

He felt shaken by his reaction at seeing Anna. A devastating mix of need and loathing had hurtled unchecked through his body, filling him with fury that he could actually lust after such a mean-spirited woman. He shouldn't feel like this. Not after all this time.

'Ogling the local peasantry isn't your style,' murmured Camilla in amusement.

He took in a long breath to steady the cascading waterfall of feelings that had knocked him off balance. Hell. Why should his guts melt at the sight of the woman? Had Anna's blistering scorn turned him into a masochist? Or a pervert? Was he really aroused by a woman who despised him? He scowled. He just wanted to be normal. To fall in love. Have kids.

'I think that's Anna,' he said, managing to find a clipped tone.

'Oh. Well, if you're going to give her a tongue-lashing, make it quick.'

Camilla looked at him fondly and touched his arm. It took all his will-power not to push her hand away and he was appalled by his irrational response to her affectionate gesture.

'I just want a word or two,' he pushed out.

With difficulty he conquered the evil little voice in his head that told him he wanted a devil of a lot more than that. Seeing Anna had kick-started his dormant libido into life. And how! Every bone he possessed ached to have

Anna sighing beneath him. For that fabulous body to be arching with pleasure.

His eyes blazed with an intense anger as he sought to crush the sexual hunger that had hit him like a hammer blow. Common sense told him that his emotional wires had become crossed. It was said that you never forgot your first love and, hell, was that true with him.

This was the spiteful little cat who'd called him promiscuous and asked coldly if he intended to infect every female in the county with some sexual disease. She'd hurled insults at him till he'd reeled. And had deliberately made him into a criminal in everyone's eyes. *Maledizione!*

With his malevolent gaze on her, his body fired with lust and loathing, he made himself saunter slowly to the picket fence. Oblivious of him, she continued to weed the handkerchief-sized front garden.

After a moment she straightened, still with her back to him. His stomach cramped. Her figure was even more womanly than before. Long, slender legs, tanned to a soft gold, the skin gleaming and flawless. Curvy hips. Tiny rear squashed temptingly in a pair of too-tight shorts that defined each buttock. Neat waist...

All too vividly he remembered being teased by his amused friends who'd suggested he put a bag over her head so he could enjoy the rest of her admittedly great body.

But because of her reserve, she had never let him anywhere near those proud, high breasts. The sublime length of those smooth legs had never wrapped around him seductively, as they had in his wild dreams.

Impatiently he struggled to master his destructive passions. His priority was to deal with the cloud that was hanging over the Pascali name. She was living yards from where he meant to set up his business. That could mean trouble. If word got around that his character was suspect, it would seriously affect his business. She could do a great deal of harm with her wicked little tongue.

The liquid sound of birdsong filled the air. He could feel the atmosphere thickening as his simmering hatred continued to pour out in her direction.

After a moment his aggression imprinted itself on her. He wasn't surprised. His loathing could have pulverised a tank.

Stiffening, she turned around warily. Her response was all that he could have wanted.

'*Vido!*' she gasped in horror.

Stunned at seeing him, she shrank back, thrown almost off balance by the sheer physical threat that emanated from his angry body. And something else even more devastating. He was projecting a raw and primitive sexuality that slammed into her gut and left her weak and breathless.

But it meant nothing. He'd always been testosterone on legs. A highly sexed male who treated women as objects for his pleasure. Her fear turned to scorn and the fine bones of her face grew taut with contempt.

Shock went through him too in violent waves, though for a different reason entirely. Expert plastic surgery had transformed her face and now she looked heart-stoppingly beautiful. All he wanted to do was to gaze at her as if he were still a lovesick fool, until the dizziness in his head subsided.

Her skin glowed with a healthy tan, her huge grey eyes sparkled. A blast of heat shot through him. A delicious feeling and one he'd forgotten.

And then her hand covered her nose as it always had whenever anyone had looked at her. His heart jerked. The gesture made him feel profoundly protective of her again, all the old sympathies crowding in on him in a swell of compassion. Grimly he reminded himself that they were wasted on her.

Once he'd believed that she'd been a poor little rich girl with no one to love her. With her parents dead and her grandfather showing her no affection, he'd felt anger on her behalf. But not for long.

His lip curled. It had been her unlovable temperament that had left her bereft of friends. She'd inherited her grandfather's cold and un-feeling nature; his hatred of his fellow man—and woman. He scowled. Whatever physical alterations Anna had made on the outside, she wouldn't have changed her malicious inner na-ture.

'Anna,' he said, his voice harsh with dislike. 'What a surprise.'

She gulped visibly and couldn't find any-thing witty or pithy to say. 'Yes.'

Vido folded his arms, adopting a dominant pose. Anna found it hard not to be intimidated. Harder still to ignore the fizz of excitement that had ripped through her in response to the simmering darkness of his hot, assessing eyes. But she couldn't prevent the worrying throb of pulses in a place she'd believed to be immune to stimulation.

It was the memories, of course. Good and bad. But why was she only recalling the good moments they'd shared? Holding hands, the laughter and companionship that had transformed her lonely life, the precious, stolen kisses…

Sternly she made herself remember the humiliation that had torn at her like a ravening tiger. When she'd realised that she was just a potential source of income to him, it had felt as if he'd crushed her vulnerable heart in his fist.

In the tense silence, she studied him warily, waiting for him to speak. His hair was a paler gold than before and beautifully cut. He looked more Italian than ever, perhaps because of the stylish linen suit and air of prosperity. His clothes seemed to murmur 'expensive' and 'classy' in hushed and reverential tones.

And yes, he was still the same as in her restless dreams. As beautiful as a young Roman god, the same golden male with that extraordinary combination of fair hair and dark, soulful eyes with their curtains of black lashes. But now there was a new air of menace about him that made her tremble.

Nervously she remembered his fury when they'd parted. It would be wise to heed her grandfather's warning about Vido's twisted, criminal mind. Her heart began to thump in time with her deep pulses.

'What are you doing here?' she asked coolly.

'Travelling to London,' he drawled.

Relief washed in waves through to her very bones. This was a chance meeting, then. For one awful moment, she'd been afraid that he'd returned to Shottery in order to plague her life!

Following the arrogant jerk of his honey-haired head, she saw a stunning blonde in a wickedly gleaming silver car, its lines almost as voluptuous as those of the woman inside it. The blonde gave a rather mocking smile, which unsettled her, and by force of habit she immediately retreated into her shell of cold reserve.

'I suggest you keep going. Your friend is waiting,' she said in pointed dismissal.

Half turning, she tried to block out the rush of emotions beginning to fill her head. She cursed the fact that he could arouse her passions as if he'd never deceived her, had never latched on to her as his route to idle riches. She burned with anger. He'd believed that she was so ugly she'd be glad of his attentions. But she'd sussed him out.

His mother had lost her job at Stanford House because of insolence. Vido had gone off the rails, staying out all night with women—according to the girls at school—and coming home in the early hours too exhausted to bother with school work. He'd been certain to win a university place but his grades had suffered because of his preoccupation with sex.

And then he'd set his sights on an easy path to riches—a pathetically grateful, love-starved idiot who'd inherit a fortune one day. What a fool she'd been.

'Camilla will wait as long as necessary,' he growled.

Arrogant chauvinist! She glared at him and wished she hadn't. The scouring desire in his eyes was unsettling. The sensual curve of his mouth, his totally sexual stance and the way the tip of his tongue touched his lips, all were deeply disturbing to her senses.

It infuriated her that she knew all his faults but her body was disregarding them. Without consulting her it had ignited with a shameful desire.

Appalled at herself, she tightened every inch and willed herself to remember the pain he'd caused her, and how because of him she'd lost even the little self-esteem she'd possessed. His betrayal had turned her into a nun, a hermit, and a crushed cabbage of a woman who'd slunk about living only half a life.

'I pity your friend. You haven't changed your attitude to women, have you?' she observed, sweeping scornful eyes up his too-perfect body. Lean and honed, she noted, then pulled herself together. A velvet-tongued, slippery Casanova, she amended. 'Women are still playthings to you,' she added in disgust.

Anger heated his blood and made it boil. She still came out with wild accusations, totally without foundation. He'd make her crawl. His mouth curved at that pleasurable thought.

'One patient and understanding woman in a car doesn't make me a chauvinist,' he clipped.

'I'm really not interested,' she said icily.

'You will be,' he muttered. *'Dunque.* You live *here* now?' he drawled.

Anna flung him a look that made no effort to hide the fact that she despised every hair on his sun-bleached head. She didn't know how he had the nerve to stand there, so sublimely sure of himself, when he'd cheated and lied and was nothing better than a common criminal.

Unsettled by the potentially explosive passion and rage that hurtled through her, she buttoned her mouth and crouched down again to tug viciously at a weed, only to discover that she'd pulled out one of her favourite aquilegias. She stared at it in dismay.

'You do live here?' he persisted in a horribly pleased murmur.

He wasn't going to go away. Biting back an 'obviously!' in answer to his question, she replied in purposely stilted tones, 'I do.'

And thought suddenly of her fiancé. Of her wedding day, when she would say those very words. Peter's gentle face swam before her eyes mistily, only to be replaced by Vido's compelling features. The muscles of her stomach clenched as a shaft of fear sliced through her. Peter was unthreatening. Loved to please her. But…did she love him? Enough to live with him forever?

'Why?' Vido barked. Seeing that she didn't understand, he elaborated slowly. 'Why are you living here?'

Oh, he'd love this, she thought. 'We've sold the house.'

'Money trouble,' he purred with evident satisfaction.

Brute. Her mouth tightened. Why was he hanging around? To crow? To leer? She controlled a shiver of apprehension.

'Rather small, after the Big House, isn't it?' came Vido's warm, honeyed silk of a voice. 'If I remember, there's just one living room and one bedroom. I've been inside. I knew your gardener, you see.' His eyes became cynical. 'He was servant class, like me.'

She wouldn't be riled by his sarcasm. Contemplating a haughty retreat into the cottage, she decided that he'd see that as a victory. So she stuck it out, wishing her shorts weren't so threadbare—and short—and that her T-shirt and face weren't streaked with dirt. All that put her at a distinct disadvantage.

'It's fine.' For a midget, she thought.

'Really? Where does your grandfather sleep?' Vido drawled, horribly persistent. 'On the sofa?'

Fixing him with Arctic eyes, she replied with deliberate bluntness.

'He's in hospital. He's had a stroke. Selling the house devastated him. Satisfied?' she flung.

But she was surprised to see the arrogance of his expression switch to something like dismay. It was several seconds before he commented curtly, 'I'm sorry.'

'Like hell you are!' she scathed.

A frown drew his black brows hard together. He seemed to be thinking rapidly. 'How is he?'

'He can't speak properly and he's partially paralysed.' Not wanting any sympathy from him, she fought to control her shaky voice. 'He's tough, though.'

He nodded. 'I think the word is *hard*. So you'll be the one on the sofa,' he taunted.

She felt irritated. Of course. Where else was there? And she dreaded the moment when she and her grandfather lived together in the tiny cottage. Since his souvenir factory had closed, he wasn't the easiest person to be with.

Tension made her voice scratchy when she stared back at him over her shoulder.

'I'm sure you're not interested in my sleeping arrangements. Rescue that blonde from boredom and get out of my hair.'

His mouth twitched slightly at the corners, but he stayed his ground.

'Interesting how fate can change people's lives so dramatically. I am rich and you are poor.'

Suddenly hearing his husky murmur in her ear, she almost lost her balance. He'd come to crouch down beside her, his hot, hungry body alarmingly close to hers. Quickly she jumped up and moved away to the end of the border.

'Fate? In your case, I imagine it was some dodgy deals that bought you that flashy car and designer clothes,' she retorted, stabbing the trowel into the soil and wishing it were Vido's evil heart.

'Careful, Anna,' he said softly. 'You're straying close to slander. I made my money by my own talent and hard work.'

'Good looks? Charm? Beautifully purred lies?' she scorned. 'Or,' she added, spitting tacks, 'a more direct route like conning some stupid rich female into funding you?'

'You are one hell of a vindictive woman!' he bit.

'Does the truth hurt, Vido?' she slammed back.

She shot a glance at the woman in the car, who was yawning with obvious boredom. *That* was one high-maintenance female. The car must have cost a fortune. Thoughtfully she studied Vido, ignoring his blistering scowl and tight jaw.

His clothes were expensive and he gave off an air of a man who spent a lot of money on being immaculately groomed and turned out. She wondered if the woman *was* the source of his income. It wouldn't be the first time he'd been prepared to sell himself for money. She felt sick at the thought.

'Get out of here,' she muttered in loathing.

'When I'm good and ready. I want to know... How does it feel to be poor, Anna?' he enquired.

'You should know,' she clipped, deadheading an early rose and wishing she could eliminate him with the same ease.

She hated feeling like this. All churned up and tense. Any minute now and she'd really lose her cool. That would really make him smirk in triumph, she thought grimly.

'Poverty is unnerving, isn't it?'

The soft and menacing passion in his voice made her twist around to see his face. His eyes had darkened ominously and yet despite his anger there was still that blatantly sexual aura about him. A delicious shudder made her nerve endings vibrate.

'Yes,' she admitted in a husky whisper. Why was he here? Why torment her like this? He was enjoying her reduced circumstances. The man was sick.

'I remember the sleepless nights,' he muttered as if on a white-hot tide of anger. 'I'd lie awake worrying about where the next penny was coming from. I'd have a sense of panic when the bills came in. And I knew that however hard I worked, I was in a trap I'd never escape.'

She shut her eyes briefly, his words reverberating in her head, and it occurred to her that he had painted *her* circumstances exactly. Being overwhelmed by the day-to-day struggle to make ends meet, she was beginning to understand—though still to condemn—his means of escaping poverty.

'Well, it looks as if you managed to get out.' She pushed back the black satin strands of hair that had fallen to half-conceal her face. She wanted him to see the depths of her contempt. 'But then,' she said steadily, 'you weren't too proud to take the money my grandfather offered for you to leave the village and me before the police caught up with you. He saved your mother from shame—and he gave you a start in life. You should be grateful to him.'

'Che Dio mi aiuti!' A terrifying fury swept his expressive features and made her shrink back in alarm. *'Grateful?!'*

The rawness of his hostility filled the air with its crackling venom. Anna felt profoundly shaken that he should hate her so much. It was clear that he didn't appreciate being reminded of his crime, she thought grimly. It didn't fit with his inflated opinion of himself.

Vido's fists clenched so hard that his nails dug sharp crescents into his palms. She didn't know. Willoughby had only told her half the story. He hadn't explained that despite being threatened with the police, he'd refused the money and told the old man to go to hell in a dustcart.

It was then that Willoughby had told him that it had been Anna who had taken the money from the factory workers' holiday fund and planted it in his locker to teach him a lesson. The old man had reminded him that it had been easy for her since she had worked every Saturday as a junior cashier in the souvenir factory.

That would have been that. Except that he'd discovered his mother weeping inconsolably. Her sister in Italy had offered them a home. For his mother's sake he had swallowed his pride and accepted Willoughby's offer of money so they could fly out and start a new life.

Going back to the old man, cap in hand, was one of the lowest moments in his entire life and he wanted to wipe it from his memory.

For a split-second he contemplated telling her all this, but he decided not to bother. She'd find out in time. Then he checked himself, frowning as he remembered Willoughby's stroke.

Dannazione! He'd wanted Anna to hear what Willoughby had said from the old man's own lips. Now what chance did he have?

He scowled in frustration. One way or another, he'd find a means to make her confess that she'd planted the money. Then he'd explain why he'd accepted Willoughby's bribe. Perhaps he could approach her a different way.

Use the highly charged sexual attraction that still, inexplicably, lay between them.

Anna watched the changing emotions on his face warily. At first she thought he was going to bluster that he was innocent, but then he checked himself and said something else that threw her off balance completely.

'Allow me to compliment you on your new nose.'

She blanched and her fingers flew to it for reassurance that he wasn't mocking her. It was an automatic reaction. She still found it hard to remember she looked relatively normal now.

'It makes you look very beautiful.' Despite the slivers of dark anger in his eyes, his tone throbbed with a carnality that swept over her like a suffocating blanket.

And her body responded with longing even while her head told her that he was playing some nasty little power game. She shuddered, fear crawling all over her.

'So I've been told,' she said flatly.

His eyebrow lifted. The downward sweep of his dark lashes alerted her to the fact that he was checking her left hand for signs of a ring. But she didn't wear it when cooking or gardening. And she wasn't going to prolong this conversation any longer.

The coldness of her silvered eyes ought to have given him frostbite. But his mouth had softened and the sensuality of his thoughtful expression slid effortlessly into her hungry body. Helpless to resist, she almost wished she still loved him. At least that would have given her an excuse for the raw, ungovernable feelings that were taking her over.

She had never ached like this. Never wanted to leap on any man—let alone Vido—and beg for sexual release. The violence of her need, and the accompanying hatred, shocked her. Mentally she was kissing the contours of his face; those raw cheekbones, the pure line of his beautiful jaw.

Had she inherited her mother's uncontrollable passions that had shocked her grandfather? She'd heard so many stories of her mother's inappropriate behaviour—though to Anna, her mother had sounded like fun.

The impromptu parties. Dancing on the lawn at midnight. Running barefoot in the snow. Kissing her father enthusiastically at every opportunity. A woman of passionate feelings that were never curbed. Was it possible to inherit such feelings?

All she knew was that her desire for Vido was running away with her, making her want to kick the traces and fling off the restraints she'd imposed on herself all these years.

The need to be physically caressed by a man—and this one in particular—was frightening her. She screwed her fingers into tight fists. Years of containment ensured that she fought through the too-enticing haze of desire that slithered into every corner of her body. And for her own self-preservation, she turned herself to stone.

'Don't keep London waiting,' she said coolly.

There was that mocking twitch of his mouth again. She felt a weird surge of excitement. It was as if he felt challenged by her and was contemplating a battle between them, to assert his will over hers.

In his dreams! Reserved though she might be, she wasn't a pushover. He'd get no satisfaction from taunting her.

Hopefully he'd get bored and go soon then she could run indoors and beat the life into some bread dough to release her pent-up anger.

And, she thought in despair, to ease the desolation of her untouched body.

'We'll meet again,' he said, his eyes dark with lustful promise.

She struggled to catch her breath. 'Not if I see you first,' she said with quiet fervour. 'This has not been a pleasure.'

'It has for me,' he murmured and the air fizzled between them setting her pulses leaping erratically. 'And it will be even more enjoyable next time. That's a promise.'

The threat alarmed her. Confused by his low, husky tone, she swivelled around so she didn't have to look at his dark and broodingly handsome face any more.

As she buried her head in a clump of blowsy daffodils, she listened hard, her breath held until her lungs were bursting. First she heard his footsteps, light and easy as he strode away. Then the thud of the car door slamming, followed by Vido's murmur and a tinkling female laugh.

Anna let out her breath in a rush of venomous loathing and gritted her teeth. He'd be gone in a moment and that would be that. An engine thrummed throatily, the sound increased in volume and then died away.

Suddenly the air seemed to clear of tension. Her scrunched-up muscles stopped screaming at her as she relaxed them. Unsteadily, she got to her feet and stumbled indoors, feeling as if she'd been caught in a washing machine on high spin. Her hands were shaking. Legs, too.

Ridiculous! He had such a terrible effect on her and for no reason at all. He had been in the wrong. She was the one who'd been his intended victim.

Wincing, she remembered how, after he'd fled to Italy, it had seemed that everyone at school had ganged up on her. She'd been bullied so unmercifully that eventually she had left school and her grandfather had grudgingly paid for private coaching.

It had been awful. Even more isolated than ever, she'd only been able to forget her unhappiness when she was cooking. And once her nose job had been successfully completed, she'd enrolled in a catering college, where she'd shone for the first time in her life.

Anna grimly scrubbed her hands and reached into the cupboard for a mug, desperate for a coffee. Preferably laced with an entire bottle of brandy, she thought ruefully.

The very core of her body ached and throbbed. It was a physical feeling entirely new to her and she hated it—hated her defencelessness against Vido's potent masculinity. It meant she was as capable of being desperate for loveless sex as Vido. And what did that make her?

Shuddering, she boiled the kettle and made her drink.

'Wretched man!' she muttered venomously, spooning in far too much sugar in her distraction. 'Just don't cross my path again. My life's enough of a hell as it is.' Too furious to think straight, she took a sip of coffee and gasped as the scalding liquid burnt her mouth. 'Damn you, Vido!' she seethed, slamming the mug down so hard that coffee splashed over her hand. She swore. And had to choke back unexpected tears.

Pain, she told herself grimly. Not misery or longing. Just anger and pain. She didn't do self-pity any more.

CHAPTER TWO

'VIDO? They're ready for you.'

Sorting a stack of papers, he nodded curtly at Camilla, who'd popped her head around his study door. 'I'll take a quick look at them.'

'Do that. You'll be fascinated,' she drawled, looking amused.

Seeing that his PA wasn't going to elaborate, he rose and headed for the office, thinking that it was good to be settled here at last.

For the past two months since he'd bought the house for Solutions Inc, the British branch of Il Conciliatore, he'd been busy in London closing down his office there and juggling his clients. At the same time, he'd been handling the renovations at his new base in Shottery by e-mail and telephone.

Most of the necessary repairs and maintenance had been completed in record time, with the exception of the kitchen—something beyond his control.

All the while he'd chafed at the delay in moving his business—mainly because he looked forward to pinning Anna down, preferably beneath him. And then under his heel. However, the matter of his good name and Anna must wait; a moment to enjoy anticipating and to relish slowly when it came.

Fired up with his usual dynamic energy, he pushed open the door to the office, which had been converted from a small anteroom. He looked around in pleasure and inhaled the scent of lilac, which filled the elegant vase on the window sill.

His priority was to appoint a decent chef now that his staff had moved in. With luck he'd find one by the end of the day. The applicants had been whittled down to a shortlist by his secretary and were comfortably settled in the drawing room with magazines and refreshments, waiting for him to interview them.

Briskly he marched to the console, which controlled the security cameras. With a flick of his finger he activated the screen. Twenty or so people sat in various attitudes of tension.

Except one. And that one in particular made him stop breathing for a moment.

'See what I mean?' Camilla smiled.

'Anna!' he muttered, his eyes as hard and as brilliant as jet.

Of course. It all came back to him. Her love of cooking, how his mother's warmth and enthusiasm had encouraged the shy, silent girl.

'The passion that's hidden in that Anna!' his mother had marvelled and he'd found himself secretly agreeing. He'd known then that the silent and reserved Anna concealed vast reserves of emotion that could match his own.

He recalled how the light had shone in her eyes when she'd released all her hidden aggression and anger on an unsuspecting heap of pasta dough. And he'd marvelled at her transparent joy as she baked and tasted, her face transformed by rapture.

It was then that he'd felt the first stirrings of desire. When her breasts were dusted with flour, her eyes sparkling with delight and her mouth soft and lush as her lips closed around a morsel of penne in salsa, the sauce leaving a tempting little smudge of scarlet on her upper lip.

Till she licked it off with sensual relish and left him a quivering mass of tormented hormones. The memory made him shift uncomfortably in the director's chair.

A chef. It figured. But...*his* chef? The very idea excited him more than he cared to admit even to himself. Yet he dismissed it out of hand. He had to think of his staff. It would be the height of madness to employ her. They both carried too much baggage and she was a spiteful little hellcat.

Though it might be amusing to put her through the interview. He found himself hoping that it might be a prelude to...other activities.

Aware of his PA's shrewd eyes on him, he took pity on his lungs and began to breathe properly again.

'Keep her till last. Don't let her see you. Get Steve to do the honours.'

With that, he swept out, hoping Camilla didn't realise that he'd wanted to feast his eyes on Anna while she sat there unaware that she was being observed.

Throughout all the interviews, her image remained in his head. Her dark hair had been neatly smoothed into a chignon that shone like a sheet of black glass. The delicate beauty of her face had made her stand out from all the others—to say nothing of her calm composure.

She'd been quietly reading one of the cookery books he'd deliberately left on the table, her expression rapt. All the others were restlessly flicking through magazines—fashion or cars, depending on their sex.

It hadn't escaped his notice that he wasn't the only one eyeing her fabulous legs, which were smooth and straight, tucked primly to one side and looking even longer than ever with the addition of high-heeled shoes. Several of the male applicants had been mesmerised too.

Vido bade an abrupt farewell to a hopeful chef whose CV was almost as fanciful as a science fiction novel. Disappointingly, no one had lived up to his high expectations and only Anna remained to be seen. A wasted day, then.

His stomach clenched as he buzzed on the intercom. 'Next one, Steve.' The tightness in his chest intensified and he wondered wryly if his digestion would cope with the stress.

Thirty seconds max to pull himself together. His gaze drifted to the picture of his late mother on his desk. He deliberately made himself remember her shame and horror when she'd learned he'd been branded a thief. His mind went back to that terrible moment when he'd walked the length of the factory floor from Willoughby's office, meeting a wall of hatred from the employees. Their curses had rained down on him. Then they'd spat in his face and flung paint at him for attempting to rob them of their hard-earned savings. It was then that he'd sworn to take his revenge on the Willoughbys one day and to redeem his honour.

To his relief, he found that his hunger for Anna had subsided. He was himself again; the tireless, driven businessman reputedly with a heart of gold beneath the grim exterior, who had forged a successful team in which even the most modestly paid employee had an equal input.

But there would be no chef to join that happy gang today. He let out an irritable sigh.

Not one of the applicants would have fitted into the tightly knit group. That meant further advertising—and in the meantime they'd have to exist on bought-in meals, when he was longing for home cooking. He scowled in frustration.

Anna waited, fidgeting now in the empty room. She had felt more and more nervous as a cheerful, casually dressed young man had collected her fellow applicants. One by one they had left, never to return, till she was the only one remaining.

She and a couple of others waiting to be interviewed had been given a sandwich lunch—from the local pub—and strawberries that were probably from the garden. During the long wait she'd read a marvellous cookery book from cover to cover and put it down with a sigh of regret, her head teeming with ideas.

All she could do now was to surreptitiously admire the redecorated, refurbished drawing room. In a palette of cool beiges and white, with occasional splashes of eau-de-Nil and turquoise, the room gave off an air of understated luxury and comfort, the fabrics oozing sensuality.

It was wonderful to be back in the house. Her heart had lifted with joy the moment she'd walked in the door to see that the interior had been transformed.

Here in this room, heavily draped curtains pooled on the thick carpet and framed the floor-to-ceiling windows. The elegant period furniture was of the highest quality, the satiny wood inviting her touch.

Flowers from the garden burst in exuberant displays from stylish vases, their perfumes wafting across the room with a heady fragrance. She loved it. The new owners had enviable taste—

'Miss Willoughby?'

This was it. Heart fluttering in time with the butterflies in her stomach, she jumped up and followed the young man who took her to the panelled hall.

'I'm Steve. General dogsbody,' he said with a friendly grin.

'Anna. Pizza cook in Stratford and ditto,' she ventured with an answering smile.

'Welcome to our paradise on earth,' he said with genuine enthusiasm. 'It's a great place to be. And good luck.'

'Thanks, I need it,' she said gratefully, comforted a little by Steve's glowing assessment of the company.

This was so important to her. A two-bedroomed apartment came with the job, which would allow her to live in comfort with her grandfather. And he'd been touchingly moist-eyed to think that he might walk in his beloved gardens again. She desperately wanted the job for his sake.

It was important to Peter, too. Her fiancé had spent ages coaching her in high-powered interview techniques. According to him,

Solutions Inc was *the* troubleshooting company to be with. It had a fantastic reputation in business and employee relations and Peter was mad keen for her to work for them.

It would, he'd said, give him a better chance to get on their pay roll himself, an ambition he'd harboured ever since the company had hit the London scene. And for her, of course, it would be a high-profile job with money to match, one she'd dreamed of for years.

'Don't be nervous,' said the young man sympathetically, pausing in the hall.

'Help! Does it show that much?' she asked in panic.

'It's the whites of your eyes that's the give-away,' he teased and she found a shaky grin. 'Take deep breaths.' Steve waited, seeming to be in no hurry. 'Better?'

She nodded and said as they strolled on, 'Marginally! I'm no longer frantic. Just Richter scale four on the earthquake gauge. My hands are shaking enough to demolish an entire building all on their own. I want this job very badly, you see.'

He laughed in delight. 'Good for you! Hope you get it. Here we are.'

They stopped outside her grandfather's old study, where Steve knocked, and pushed open the door for her. It was an odd feeling to be here again, in an entirely different capacity. Heiress to employee in one bound, she thought, her smile rueful now.

'That's it. Smile away. Mr Pascali likes us to be happy,' Steve confided.

She blinked at the young man, wondering if she'd heard him properly. It felt as if she'd been dropped down an elevator shaft in a twenty-storey building.

'Pascali?' she whispered, white-faced, wondering if she'd ever get her stomach back to where it belonged.

'Sure,' he whispered back. 'Half-Italian. Comes from Milan. But calm down. He's great. Won't bite, honest. He doesn't smile a lot and he's tough and drives himself hard but he's fair. And so long as we don't throw ''sickies'', he's great when we're really ill. A star, through and through.'

That didn't sound like Vido. A star? A matter of opinion, she thought tartly and would have turned tail and run, but by then the young man had pushed her inside and shut the door behind her.

Immediately her defences went up. Looking around the wonderfully light and airy study, its once half-empty wall shelves now filled with books, her wary gaze alighted on Vido where he sat behind a vast mahogany desk.

Without warning, her body moved into meltdown. He looked sensational. He was wearing a Wedgwood-blue waistcoat and co-ordinating shirt, its sleeves neatly rolled back to reveal muscular arms, and an expression that could only be described as that of a predatory panther, poised to strike after a long period of fasting.

She swallowed, confused, forgetting Peter's instruction to march in and take charge, to pretend that she had a natural confidence and assurance. But they'd both known she wasn't like that. And even less so, with Vido's ruthlessly assessing gaze stripping her right down to the bone.

Her head swam as his liquid dark eyes turned her from professional chef in interview mode to all-woman. She didn't have time to think. Her mind was too busy dealing with the gloriously sensual sensations that were bringing her alive.

Fight or flight. She must concentrate. There was but a second or two to choose. Of course it was inconceivable that she'd get the job, even if she wanted to work for a man she utterly despised. She'd be wasting her time if she stayed another moment.

The trouble was that if she left now it would be seen as the act of a coward, someone who was scared of him. Her mouth firmed in resolution. Hell would freeze over before she let him know how strongly he affected her. It was fight, then.

'Anna. Welcome to my home.'

Despite the lascivious thoughts exploding in his head, he'd managed to rise, his tone deliberately mocking. As he extended his hand, Anna checked her loose-limbed stride. It seemed his assertion that he was now the master of Stanford House had thrown her completely off balance. He smiled faintly with satisfaction.

'Vido.'

Her husky whisper ricocheted through some alarmingly sensitive parts of him. More tantalisingly, she licked her lips and he realised that she must be dry-mouthed in shock. Swallowing, and as if driven by an involuntary action she couldn't prevent, she hesitantly walked towards him then reached out to allow his hand to close around hers.

He knew he'd hung on to her a shade too long. But that was because her grave grey eyes were fixed on his in hurt dismay and his mind had momentarily gone blank.

His protective instincts were urging him to leap over the desk and soothe her agitation. Which only showed how stupid and unreliable one's instincts could be. Anna was pure ice and acid lemon through and through to her cold little steely heart.

Snatching her hand away and rubbing her palm as if he'd burnt it, she snapped without preamble, 'When did you know I'd applied for this job?'

She was stunning in her anger. Eyes blazing. A flush on those high cheekbones. Her ribcage high with those short inhalations of breath. Glorious. He gritted his teeth against the urge to catch her to him and fling her down on his desk. Later, he promised himself. And had to stop himself from gasping at the shaft of pleasure that gave him.

'Not till this morning,' he managed, sounding harsher than he'd intended.

She bristled. 'And yet knowing that, you kept me waiting all day.'

He allowed himself a small smile. Fortunately she didn't know how much that wait had cost him. Tension had mounted as each applicant came and went. And now his self-control was all over the place, scattering at the very nearness of her. Seducing her promised to be one hell of a way to begin his vendetta.

'That's right.'

He was breathing too heavily. A drowsy lassitude was stealing over him and he silently cursed her for what she was doing to his body. A bad dose of old-fashioned lust. Fine—but he needed to stay in control.

There was a sizzling flash as her eyes registered contempt.

'Petty of you,' she spat.

'Or perhaps I wanted to see you last so that we could have a long chat.' He waited for her comment but she merely glared. 'What do you think of the renovations?' he probed, seeking something banal to cool his ardour and reduce it to mere boiling point.

She hesitated. 'It pains me to say it but they're wonderful,' she said, her tone grudging. 'You've returned the house to its former glory.'

It was a gracious concession and one that surprised him. He acknowledged her compliment with a dip of his head.

'It gave me a lot of pleasure to do so,' he murmured.

'I bet,' she muttered.

'Please sit down,' he drawled, enjoying the elegance of her fluid movements as she sank rather suddenly into the high-backed Georgian chair, almost as if her legs would no longer support her.

Studying her, he saw that her charcoal-grey suit was well tailored and decided that it must have been part of her wardrobe before the Willoughbys had discovered the reality of poverty. Her white shirt was impeccable and ironed to within an inch of its life but the cuffs were a little frayed.

Seeing his gaze linger on her wrists, she blushed and drew her hands back into the sleeves of the jacket. A woman who blushed at the age of twenty-six! he marvelled. And felt distinctly unsettled by that.

'I knew we'd meet again, but I didn't expect it to be like this,' he opened lazily.

Her chin jerked up to reveal a defiant mouth. 'I thought I'd seen the last of *you*.' Her tone suggested that it had been her fervent hope, too. 'I don't even know why I'm still sitting here,' she muttered.

He admired her spirit—and again her honesty. She'd made no concession to the fact that she ought to be trying to please her prospective employer. The idea of having her working here ignited him. No. It was impossible. Forget it.

'Curiosity and destiny perhaps. We have unfinished business,' he drawled.

'That's where you're wrong!' she retorted. 'The past is over and done with.'

If only, he thought. But he had scores to settle. Questions that had to be answered. A vow to fulfil. A delicious sense of triumph rolled through him.

'It might have been. Except that I have now moved close to where you live and so the past can't be ignored. Every time I see you or pass your cottage, I will think of what happened between us,' he purred.

'Nothing happened!' she protested. 'I made sure of that.'

That was her take on it. But his life, and his mother's, had been turned upside down by the Willoughbys. His mouth thinned.

'Oh, a great deal happened, Anna,' he growled. 'Believe me, it did.'

As if remembering the early, golden days they'd spent together, she touched her mouth with a nervous finger and he found himself recalling the pressure of her warm, sensual lips and the melting of her body against his.

He noticed her breasts rise and fall quickly as if the memory bothered her too.

'I—I didn't know you'd bought the house. I had no idea you were behind the consortium or I'd never have come,' she muttered defensively, her mouth shaping into such a soft pout that it pushed his physical tension to new heights.

He had never wanted anyone so badly. Every time he looked at her he felt a raw, primitive urge that seemed hell bent on consuming him.

'Are you saying it makes a difference to your application because I'm the boss here?' he asked softly.

'You know it does,' she said jerkily, wrapping her arms defensively around herself. 'I'd never work for a guy like you, not in a million years.' Disappointment touched the corners of her mouth. 'I might have had a chance with someone else interviewing me,' she muttered resentfully.

He felt the urge to employ her, to keep her close. An ache skewered his loins. Be rational, he cautioned himself. The way he felt about her, this hunger and the loathing that accompanied it, was no basis on which to introduce her to his easygoing and hard-working staff. They didn't deserve to be pitched into the middle of a potentially explosive situation.

Or to be saddled with a class-conscious colleague who felt superior to almost everyone. She'd never accept the cleaner or the gardener as her equal.

This conversation, then, was just for his amusement. Before he went for the kill, got her into his bed then extracted an admission of her guilt and an abject apology from her. After which, he'd wipe her from his life once and for all.

'You're suggesting I'd be biased against you?' he queried, idly marvelling at the flawlessness of her pale-gold skin. Was she like that all over? Pulses thundered in his ears. He'd find out soon.

'Of course you would be.'

He brought his mind back, annoyed by its wandering. She uncrossed her legs, the movement suggesting that she was preparing to leave. But he wanted to keep her there as long as possible. To enjoy the new experience of his revitalised libido in the hope that it might remain hot and eager when she went and he could behave in future like any red-blooded male.

'I can assure you,' he drawled with absolute truth, 'that landing this job depends on how you'd fit in and whether your cooking skills are suitable.'

She blinked in astonishment. 'But...' She licked her lips and his hypnotised gaze focused on their pink softness as he imagined the taste of her. When her lips parted to allow him a glimpse of her small, perfect teeth, he almost groaned aloud. And cursed her. Admittedly he was enjoying the novelty of his arousal. But not if he couldn't keep a clear head. 'You're mad. We...couldn't work together!' she declared breathily.

'Together? Hardly that. It wouldn't be an *intimate* association,' he murmured, blotting out some highly salacious thoughts. Her in the kitchen. Him, creeping up and... Hell. He squeezed his thighs together tightly and got back on course. 'You'd be cooking. I'd be eating,' he added drily.

Why the devil, he wondered, was he playing around like this? He ought to be throwing her application right back at her and consoling her with a different offer entirely.

And yet...some stubborn part of him—the male, testosterone-filled part that had been sadly neglected for years—couldn't resist the idea of having her working as his chef. His mind raced on. *Santo cielo!* Was he mad? No. Just starved of fantastic sex. But he could have that, he felt sure. He didn't have to employ her as well.

Pulling himself together—*again!*—he fumbled around in his befuddled mind for a neutral question. In a neutral tone, if he could manage it.

'I'm curious to know why you applied.'

Her eyes filled with scorn. 'Vido, is there any point in either of us wasting our time on this farce?'

'Could be,' he conceded, going totally against common sense. 'Do you want the job?'

'I *did*.'

Yes. Definite disappointment. He felt a kick of excitement. 'Am I to understand that you definitely wouldn't work here because of me?'

Her eyes widened as if he'd said something unbelievably stupid. Which he probably had. She took a deep breath, her eyes scalding.

'Are you joking?' she scathed. And then, almost to herself, 'I really liked the sound of this job. It was everything I've ever wanted.'

'But.'

Her eyes lowered and he found his gaze focusing on her lush mouth. Very kissable. A lying, deceitful mouth that tasted of honey.

'Yes,' she croaked. 'And it's a pretty enormous "but", isn't it?'

His mind was suddenly racing with possibilities. Under the circumstances, he couldn't put pressure on the ailing Willoughby to admit that he'd confessed Anna had slipped the money into the locker. But perhaps he had found the ideal way to put the screws on *her*. He felt a load lift from his shoulders. Yes. That was it.

Two things were bugging him. The terrible need he felt for her, and the fact that she could easily spread malicious gossip about his good character. His reputation had been built on honesty and trust. It was essential he should be whiter than white. Anna must be silenced. And what better way than to have her both in his employ and in his bed?

He'd take her on. Seduce her too. His heart pumped faster. Then he'd trap her into an admission while she was in the throes of passion. And get the confession he needed.

CHAPTER THREE

VIDO let his mind spin through the obvious—if crazy—conclusion. There would be side benefits, he reasoned. If she spent time with him here, she'd also discover the kind of man he really was. She'd come to question her mistaken judgement of him.

After working here for a while, she'd know without a shadow of doubt that truth and honour were part and parcel of his nature and she'd be ready to listen to his side of the story.

Why that was important to him, he didn't know. Only that it was.

She'd have to apologise for her insults and her vindictive behaviour on her knees…

He almost let out a groan, picturing the moment, wondering what stage their relationship would have reached by then. Would she, by then, be begging for his favours as well—or begging for them to continue?

He couldn't deny that seducing her would give him pleasure. Every rampant, demanding hormone in his body was telling him that. Her capitulation would be even sweeter accompanied by fulsome apologies.

And then he'd be free of her. Free to settle down with a warm and affectionate woman like Camilla, someone who'd love him and give him healthy children without hang-ups. His PA was out of the picture now, since she'd fallen heavily for the gardener, but...

'I think we've come to a full stop, don't you?' she said suddenly.

He gave a quick frown, realising that he'd been silent for too long. 'No. More of a comma.' At her raised eyebrow, he scratched around for a reason and alighted on one in relief. 'If I don't interview you properly, you would be entitled to complain and sue for discrimination. That would be a disaster. My companies have a reputation for fairness second to none.'

He paused, fighting the urge to tell her that staff agencies told him his company was so popular and sought-after that applicants would sell their grandmothers into slavery to work for him. She'd never believe that.

'*Really?*' she said coolly.

As expected, she didn't give credence to a word he'd said.

His eyes narrowed, the line of his mouth tightening in anger at her contempt for him. On her knees, he vowed, his eyes glinting. She would learn that it was possible to be poor and honest and he'd never had designs on her inheritance.

He reckoned that his staff could cope with her snobbery for, say...six months max. They'd show her how people from all walks of life could contribute. How well they could get on. She needed that lesson. His mind turned to steel.

'Ask around,' he growled, offended by her tone. 'I'm known to be just and generous to my employees and I don't want that reputation questioned. So let's continue as if we've never met before. First,' he said, sweeping on before she could claim that was an impossible task, 'I'll tell you a little about the company and myself. Then you can explain why you initially wanted to work here. After that, we'll go through the usual rigmarole. I'm legally bound to do this. Understood?'

Her eyes were a soft, cloudy grey that did their best to disconcert him with their look of naked apprehension. Wary and suspicious, she appeared to consider her options. He pretended to be indifferent even though he could hear his heart thudding hard and fast with anticipation.

He needed her consent. It was imperative that she entered his web and became tangled in it. How long he kept her after that was a matter of conjecture.

She knew that this was her chance to leave with her dignity unimpaired. But for some time she had been shaking too much to risk getting to her feet. The power of him, the almost hypnotic quality of his black, fevered eyes, had kept her glued to the chair.

She dared not move. So she shrugged as if she didn't care either way what she did and handed over her CV.

Vido pretended to study it even though the words swam around like tadpoles.

'I have nothing to lose, have I?' The smoky eyes, fringed with impossibly black lashes, met his in icy challenge. 'Go on. I'm intrigued. Tell me about yourself. Explain how you made your money with your own *talent*.'

From her scathing tone, she made it sound as if he'd opened up a string of brothels funded by a weekly drug run from Colombia.

Leaning back in his chair, he suppressed his rising temper. It would give him great pleasure to see her humbled.

'I'll stick to describing my current achievements,' he said coldly. 'You don't need to know how I got to my present position.'

'Ashamed of what you did?' she wondered aloud.

Bitch. His jaw tightened. The need for justice burned deeper with every insult she flung at him.

'No. It's too long a story. But you'll hear it one day, you can be sure of that,' he replied through his teeth. 'For the moment you'll have to be satisfied with information on a need-to-know basis. I've built my reputation as a troubleshooter,' he continued, launching grim-faced into his spiel. 'When businesses get into difficulties, I turn around their falling sales, solve battles between the staff, and put the businesses back into profit. My job is to say the unsayable, transform teams, and sort out rivalries and power struggles so that a business can function as it should.'

Suddenly she seemed very attentive. Almost fascinated. He continued, trying not to over-

egg the pudding. Just the facts, he told himself.
For now.

'I have a company in Milan—Il
Conciliatore, which means troubleshooter.
Two years ago I started up a sister company
based in London, which is in the process of
moving here—'

'Why?' she shot with icy directness.

Seeing the suspicion in her eyes, he gave a
mocking smile. 'I had to go somewhere,' he
replied. 'It's the heart of England, a good place
to be for my business. Besides, I knew how
beautiful it was around the Stratford area. And
I have always regarded this village as home.'
He let that sink in. 'I particularly wanted a
good quality of life for my employees and their
families. Don't get the wrong idea. I'm not a
soft touch—'

'I wouldn't dream of thinking you were,'
she said with feeling.

He narrowed his eyes. With every sarcastic
utterance she made, her hatred fuelled his need
to win this particular battle. He'd crush her.
Mentally, emotionally, physically.

'It's wise business practice,' he said tightly.
'People work better when they're happy. I get

more out of them and sick leave is cut to a minimum.'

'So we've established you like to work your employees hard, while they fondly imagine you're benevolent,' she said with an unlikely sweetness. 'But why Stanford House?'

Persistent little madam. 'I needed a large country house for my purpose,' he answered, omitting to mention that there had been several others, which would have been just as suitable.

'And acquiring it gave you a nice little revenge,' she said, her lip curling. Her direct gaze challenged him to deny that.

So he didn't. 'Of course. It was quite a moment,' he conceded, provoked further by the glitter of steel in her intense grey eyes. 'You can't blame me. Many years ago, I stood here in this very room, pleading on my mother's behalf and explaining that she'd complained to your grandfather because he'd made her work five days' overtime for no extra pay. It wasn't right that he'd sacked her just for that. However, I swallowed my pride and begged him to reinstate her because she desperately needed the money. He sat where I'm sitting now and laughed at me. Called me...' he took a breath to ease his starved lungs '...a sniv-elling little bastard son of a whore.'

Anna gave a little gasp. Remembering that moment, he could feel the skin tautening over his cheekbones. His nostrils flared and whit-ened.

'I was dragged away by two heavies and thrown out. By the back door, of course. Not the front,' he added softly. But his anger spat sparks from every carefully enunciated word.

'I'm sorry about that. Grandpa was very...Victorian where his staff were con-cerned.' Anna had the grace to look uncom-fortable before she rallied. 'But don't forget, he's in hospital because of the house sale,' she said in retaliation.

'What exactly are you suggesting? If you think about it,' he clipped, 'it was his bad man-agement which made the disposal of the house necessary. In fact, I realised that the factory was in trouble ten years ago. Staff relations were at an all-time low even then. My role in the purchase of the house had nothing to do with his stroke. I came along at the right mo-ment and paid a good price, relieving his debt considerably. Your grandfather's illness was not of my making. Was it?' he demanded, flinging the words at her like pistol shots.

'No.' Contrite, she looked down at her hands, which were twisting restlessly on her lap. 'I apologise if I implied it was. And he shouldn't have been so rude to you. I didn't know about that.'

'Apology accepted,' he bit, not relaxing for one moment.

Sullen and rebellious, her eyes flashed up to his. 'So why do you need a house like this instead of a large office block?'

'It's the way I work,' he replied shortly. 'I intend to continue the methods that produced so many successes in Milan. We assess the state of our clients' companies on site. Then I intend to bring the management here—and anyone else concerned—for a long weekend. Whilst off duty and enjoying various relaxing leisure activities, the managers will reveal a good deal about themselves. It's an essential part of understanding how they interact and re-act to one another.'

'Your *staff* are involved in this?'

With a frown drawing her dark brows to-gether, she leant forward, clearly intrigued. Fascination had parted her lips and her eyes sparkled with interest. Her skin seemed to glow.

Damn her. Hopelessly diverted, he stared at her CV and made a totally unnecessary mark beside some of the bullet points. He needed to stay sharp and focused if he was to steer her towards accepting his offer.

'Anyone with an opinion will be welcome to air it. We all eat breakfast and lunch together and chat things over. Me, our guests, my PA, secretary, gardener, handyman, fellow troubleshooters and...the chef.' She'd be dynamite amongst that lot, he thought. He wrestled with his conscience. And lost. He had to have her here. To bow her to his will. 'We work as one unit. Everyone pulls together. That's why I spend so long on choosing my employees.'

Her eyebrow shot up, a touch of wry humour lifting her mouth. 'That lets me out.'

Temper caught him. 'Because you think you're far too well-bred to consort with my handyman and gardener?'

'No. Because you're doing the choosing and I'd be bottom of your list after slugs and snails,' she countered. 'Well, thanks for your valuable time. I'm off.'

'You'll stay right where you are!' he ordered, the authority in his voice pinning her to the seat. 'I am obliged to give you a fair crack of the whip and you're not going till this interview is finished. Your turn.' Seeing he'd stopped her in her tracks, he allowed himself a small smile. 'Sell yourself to me,' he murmured.

It was a definite challenge and he looked at her with a hint of mocking arrogance in his expression.

That small smirk decided it for her. With her legs no longer pretending to be wobbling jellies, she'd been on the point of walking out. Instead, she'd dazzle him with her brilliance and make him wish he could employ her.

With no chance of that happening, she might as well use this interview as a practice run for others. With a little shrug, she settled herself more comfortably in her chair and tried to remember the opening words that Peter had written for her to say.

'I'm a qualified chef, as you can see from my CV,' she began. 'When I left my catering course as the top student in the college, I had an offer to work as a sous chef in a well-known London restaurant. This was highly unusual, but the college principal personally recommended me and once I'd worked a trial day at the restaurant, the chef asked me to stay on. My cooking and kitchen organisation skills, I was told, are outstanding—'

'Which restaurant?'

'La Scala,' she said with some pride. 'You have the chef's reference there.'

Vido looked impressed, as well he might. All the celebrities flocked there and the chef was a famous personality in his own right. She was disappointed, though, that he didn't bother to read the glowing reference.

'You were there for three years. Then, I see, you were head chef in Georgio's, in Stratford. Something of a comedown. And...currently,' he purred, after hastily checking her CV, 'you're cooking pizzas.' His eyes were mocking. 'Presumably you weren't up to those jobs after all.'

'On the contrary. I did them standing on my head,' she said coldly.

'Messy, when preparing soup,' he commented.

A smile escaped before she could kill it. A flash of their past banter went through her head. They'd had such fun. She winced. The whole time, he'd been secretly laughing at her gullibility.

She'd been incredibly ugly, scorned by everyone and the butt of constant jokes. Scared and intimidated by the bullies, she'd crept about school like a frightened mouse and rarely opened her mouth. Why had she ever imagined that someone as desirable as Vido would choose to be with someone so repulsive?

'Ha ha,' she said without an ounce of humour.

Vido leaned forwards, his eyes intent on her taut face. 'OK. Why did you leave La Scala?'

Pain flickered in her eyes at the memory of that terrible moment when her ambition had been thwarted. But she rallied.

'I had to return to Stratford because Grandpa's factory was in trouble by then and he needed me around.'

By the frown that drew his brows together, he seemed affronted by her explanation. 'You're telling me that you turned down the prospect of a glittering career for his convenience?'

'I had to.' Her mouth took on a stubborn line.

'So that your grandfather could come home to vent his spleen on you? So he could be served a cooked meal before he drowned his sorrows in a bottle of malt whisky?'

She flushed. Vido had described the situation with biting accuracy. 'He needed me. I couldn't desert him,' she said stiffly.

Vido scowled. 'You needed your own life, your own future. Talent should never be wasted. He's a selfish old man and should have allowed you to—'

'I couldn't leave him to cope alone!' she said indignantly. 'Would you have left your mother like that?'

He jerked back in his seat. Then glared. 'No.'

'Well, then.'

'But my mother had cared for me,' he said softly. 'Loved me. Worked day and night for my benefit—'

'My grandfather had to give up a lot to bring me up—'

'Is that true? I got the impression that you just had to fit in with his life the best you could.'

'I'm not discussing him with you,' she bit. 'You're exceeding the needs of this interview.

All you need to know is that I am an experienced chef and the only reason I don't have a restaurant of my own is because I have to stay close to home. I was forced to leave Georgio's because the hours were so awful. And I applied for this position because I want a challenge. My present job is a waste of my skills— and frankly it's boring.'

She paused, annoyed. He was staring at her legs. She felt the intensity of his gaze almost as if his hand was caressing her with long strokes…up her shin. Around her knee. Along the inch or two of thigh exposed by her skirt.

The heavy lashes flicked up and his gaze met her eyes. She was trembling.

'You want something more exciting?' he said, his expression so unreadable that she thought she'd been imagining things.

But her body didn't feel the same way. Assailed by the tingling of her skin and the heavy beat of her heart, she'd totally lost the thread of what she was saying.

Somehow she caught her wits before they totally deserted her. Vido was all male. Ogling women was what he did as a matter of course. Nothing personal.

'Yes,' she said doggedly. 'Someone told me about this job. They'd seen it in *The London Press*—'

'Someone?' he queried, pouncing on her remark.

Anna's fingers went to her engagement ring. Vido suddenly saw this and his eyes narrowed.

'My fiancé,' she said equably, gaining confidence.

'Just got engaged?'

She remembered that she hadn't been wearing her ring the last time they'd met. 'No. Six months ago.'

She was loved. Lovable. Her brow furrowed. At least, she thought Peter loved her though he wasn't very effusive. He'd proposed, after all. He wanted a wife and children. It was a very companionable kind of relationship.

'You have plans for marriage?' Vido's harsh tone broke into her disastrously wandering thoughts.

'Of course,' she said automatically. 'In two months' time.'

So soon! Whenever she thought of it now she felt a cold chill of doubt. Her childhood and teenage years had made her vulnerable to charm—she'd proved that by falling for the deceitful Vido. Could she be making the same mistake with Peter? But before she could dwell on this, he had captured her uncertain gaze with his.

'At least you can be sure he's not a fortune-hunter,' he muttered.

She went cold. Vido had voiced something she'd been thinking for the past few months. Peter had been shocked when her grandfather had been made a bankrupt. He'd gone a sickly green.

'Peter has a well-paid job in the City,' she declared.

Vido's eyes were as hard as jet. 'Continue. You saw the advert. What attracted you most to the job?'

Disconsolately she gathered her thoughts. This could have been a dream position. If only…

She brought herself up sharp. No point in wishing. She'd get over the disappointment.

'I suppose the fact that it specified a preference for someone experienced in cooking Italian food. There's nothing I like more than preparing home-cooked meals, Italian-style—'

'You can cook *agnolotti? Ribollita? Spezzeltino?'*

'*Spezzatino,*' she corrected, wondering if he'd been testing her. 'Vido, read the references. I'm not bragging. I am a great chef where Italian food is concerned. One of the best. I'm used to presenting food to La Scala standards. That says it all, I think.'

'You could produce dinner for, say, twenty? Thirty?'

'Easy,' she said with confidence. 'I'd even worked out a few menus—'

'Let me see.'

The tone was too commanding to refuse. Digging into her bag, she removed the relevant sheets and handed them over. She'd spent hours on them. Much good may they do her, she thought.

Though they'd make good menus for Peter's clients. An image of her married self, slaving in the kitchen after work while her husband entertained his guests, flashed before her eyes. It was a future she shrank from.

There was a silence while Vido intently studied the menus. She was able to study *him* without being zapped by that intimidating stare.

The dark crescent lashes. The long, straight nose. His sexy lips which were parting in a smile of pleasure as he read. She knew how mouth-watering her choices were. But she wasn't prepared for his reaction to be so incredibly sensual.

His lazy gaze lifted to hers and it was as if all his hostility had been dropped for a moment.

'*Complimenti,*' he murmured, his voice as rich as tiramisu. 'You have successfully aroused my appetite.'

A tremor went through her even though she realised that he was referring to the enticing menus. This was how he seduced all those women, she thought, her throat dry as a desert. He gave them that slow stare and sexy drawl that made his mouth move as if it was ripe for kissing.

'That was my intention,' she replied, sounding more like nutmegs being grated.

'One you may regret,' he purred and she wondered what he meant.

Her hands fluttered. 'Why?' she croaked.

He merely smiled, as if he had private plans for her. He exuded an electric energy that seemed to hurtle towards her like a living thing that was hell bent on destroying her. And the terrible thing was that this excited her.

'I'm asking the questions for now. What else attracted you?' he shot.

She blinked, thinking of the way his lips curled with sensual intent. The sharpness of his white teeth…

'What?' she asked hazily.

The heavy lashes flickered. 'To the position…of chef.'

'Oh!' He was goading her, deliberately making sure she knew what she'd be losing by being refused the job, she thought irritably. Yet honesty compelled her to reply. 'Obviously it would be the furnished, luxury two-bedroomed flat.'

'And of course you would have had the freedom to roam the grounds of your old home in your leisure time,' he reminded her, twisting the knife with vicious relish.

Anna lowered her eyes to hide the pain. The job had seemed too good to be true. Now she knew that it *was* too good to be true.

'Grandfather would have loved being here,' she admitted grudgingly.

Vido nodded, seemingly in sympathy, but she knew better. 'Free accommodation in a place he regards as home.'

'OK!' she grated. 'You've made your point. But he would never come here, knowing you owned the house!'

'No. What a shame. It would have speeded his recovery, wouldn't it?' he said with a show of regret and she wanted to fly at him and tear her nails down his face. She checked her anger, appalled at its ferocity. 'Then there's the salary—'

'It wasn't a priority like the other things I've mentioned.' She sat stiff and resentful, hating him with all her heart.

'Though it would be generous enough to transform your lives.'

Anger splintered her self-control. 'Yes! Does that satisfy you?' she cried, stung into retaliating. 'Are you amused and pleased? Do you take pleasure in the fact that our positions are reversed? If so, you can put yourself in the same category you put my grandfather and me! You thought we looked down on people less fortunate than ourselves and now *you're* revelling in your position and virtually salivating because—'

'I wouldn't be human if I didn't feel some kind of satisfaction that justice had prevailed—'

'*Justice?* That a liar and a thief, who wouldn't know a moral if it sat on him, has conned his way up to the top?'

'How passionate you are, Anna,' he said tightly. 'And I thought you so cool and controlled.'

But not where you're concerned, she thought, the bitterness biting into her like a canker.

There was a long silence. She saw that he was studying her intently. Tension thickened the air between them and it became hard for her to breathe naturally. He dominated the room. She'd heard of people having 'presence' before—and now she knew what that meant. A charismatic energy force that sucked you towards it, however unwillingly.

And she was being drawn to him despite all her efforts to stay aloof. In panic, she looked away, afraid of his power to liquefy her brain and body.

'I think you've fulfilled your obligation to interview me,' she said coldly. Stiff with tension, she rose to her feet, willing her weak and trembling legs not to let her down. 'As far as I'm concerned there's nothing more to be said. Are you done with this farce of political correctness?'

'You think there might be more we could do?' he silked.

She felt a ripple of heat run through her and shut her mind to what she *wanted* to do with him. Horrified by the sexual ache that seemed to be taking her common sense and decency over, she replied with tight self-loathing;

'No. Just that I had expected some tough questions and role-playing.'

She wondered why she was speaking as if she was intoxicated, the words slurring alarmingly. Her frantic eyes settled on him. The light from the window was highlighting his beautiful cheekbones and she imagined pressing her lips to the dark hollows beneath. Then moving on to his gloriously carved mouth...

'We can play if you like,' he offered. 'I'm game.'

She had to swallow. The husky tone had vibrated deep in her body and she could feel herself becoming damp with desire. It was a humiliating reaction. One she'd never had with Peter.

Her mind whirled. That was wrong. They would be lovers one day. Yet the thought of physical intimacy with Peter filled her with dismay and she knew that she must sort that particular situation out. When she'd discovered where her sanity had gone.

'I'm not,' she jerked out primly. 'We've taken up enough of one another's time on a rather pointless exercise. Goodbye.'

She could barely get the final word out. A sense of utter dismay had claimed her. She had wanted the job more than she'd realised and it was harder than she could have imagined to walk away. Even from a monster like Vido.

'Anna. Wait.'

With drooping shoulders, she paused half-way to the door. He came to stand in front of her, blocking her escape.

'What now?'

She knew she'd sounded irritable, but she wanted to leave before he realised how miserable she was. And before he could discover how easily he'd aroused her. She tightened her thigh muscles and waited, grim-faced, just listening to her body throbbing and wondering why he, of all men, should be able to find his way so surely to her innermost desires.

'I would like you to meet my staff,' he murmured.

Looking up, her eyes huge and startled, she saw nothing in his implacable face to explain why.

'What on earth for?' she asked with a frown.

'Hunger.'

She glared. There were too many double meanings flying around for her liking. His mocking expression suggested they were all intentional.

'Try the chip shop.'

'Please! We're all desperate,' he coaxed, wielding his silvery tongue to devastating effect. 'I'll come clean. I badly need a chef to make my plans work to their full potential. I have people arriving next week and I don't want to feed them take-aways. You're more familiar with Italian home-cooking than anyone I've interviewed. Those menus have stimulated my gastric juices more than you can imagine.'

He could have sold central heating on the equator, she thought sourly. 'Of course. They were designed to give me an advantage over other applicants,' she muttered, resenting him.

'They did more than that. They made you irresistible.' There was a long silence that seemed to thicken the space between them. 'I have a suggestion, Anna. Cook dinner. Nothing grand, just a family kind of meal. Twelve of us altogether. If you like us and we like you—and the food—I'll give you a six-month trial.'

It was too cruel. Everything she'd dreamed of... There was a wild flutter of excitement in her stomach but she crushed it with ruthless speed before it affected her judgement. Vido wasn't to be trusted.

'Is this a ploy to get your supper cooked?' she asked scornfully.

In one swift second, Vido's face turned to granite. 'No,' he said, clearly bristling at the idea. 'It's a genuine offer.'

'Not a little game? Do you want me to tell you I want the job so that you can take a perverse delight in turning me down?' she demanded.

'You do have a bad opinion of me, don't you?' he said with soft dislike. 'You're more than qualified to be my chef. The only doubt in my mind is how you'd gel with the team. In the final analysis, the staff will decide whether they like you, not me. I have one vote. That's how we operate. As a democracy.'

Doubt shadowed her face. Vido had admitted he'd enjoyed the sensation of buying the house from her grandfather. Maybe it would be equally satisfying to employ her. Then he could sit at the head of the table and see her hot and flushed from the kitchen, dishing up food for him like a forelock-tugging menial. A horrible, petty triumph.

Her gaze fell and she surveyed her uncomfortable new shoes disconsolately. Grandpa would be so distressed to know she hadn't landed the job. He'd been sure she'd get it. Her hands clenched into fists and she tightened her jaw in frustration.

The generous salary would have enabled her to send him to the convalescent home he'd set his heart on. Instead, they'd be jammed in the little cottage, snapping at one another while she worked all hours to pay the basic bills. Horrible.

Despairing, she shut her mind to the temptation to say 'yes' and prepared herself for a few more months of spinning pizzas around. The prospect made her feel bone-weary, as if the life had been sucked out of her.

'You know it's out of the question,' she said, choking back tears of disappointment and frustration. 'We can't both be in the same house.' She lifted her chin and met his liquid eyes. 'The answer,' she snapped, biting back her misery with a superhuman effort, 'is an emphatic *no*.'

CHAPTER FOUR

STILL blocking her exit, Vido folded his brawny arms over his exquisite waistcoat. 'I'm sorry that what happened between us in the past has affected you so deeply,' he observed with a frown.

'How can you say that?' she fended, making a good job of avoiding a straight answer.

He gave a very Italian shrug of his shoulders. 'If it meant nothing, you'd see this as a great opportunity. Perhaps you are scared,' he murmured, 'that I might mistreat you as your grandfather mistreated my mother and the rest of his staff?'

Her glare would have withered a more sensitive man.

'Don't be ridiculous!' she scoffed. 'You wouldn't dare.'

Truth to tell, she was scared of herself. Of her feelings. And aghast at the way her emotions were tossed around like stir-fry in a pan whenever he fixed her with that sultry stare. Scared, too, of the raw burning inside her that was clamouring to be eased by a highly carnal hour or so with him.

'Then I don't see the problem.' Steel hardened his expression. 'Are you worried, maybe,' he mocked, 'that I might live up to the criminal record you gave me and steal the contents of your purse?'

'Not *now*,' she flung back. 'Not now that you've somehow made your fortune—'

'Surprising,' he drawled, 'how much contempt you managed to get into that word ''somehow''.'

She sucked in an angry breath. He deserved her contempt. 'Can't you see? We'd be scoring points off one another all the time. And Grandpa would never set foot in this house knowing that you now own it.'

'Ah. That is a problem,' he admitted. 'How long before he's out of hospital?'

'Next week, we hope, if things go well. If I can find the money, he'll go to a nursing home to convalesce before he comes home—'

'By which time,' Vido said, 'you'd be settled here. It's time he put your interests first. He's had a lifetime of having his own way.'

'It's useless discussing this. You talk about fitting in,' she went on sharply. 'The trouble is that I don't like you and you don't like me. That's hardly the basis for a comfortable arrangement.'

'Comfortable...?' He seemed to consider this with some amusement. 'No, it would never be that. You owe me something, Anna. For the lies, the shame, the humiliation—'

'I owe you nothing!' she declared. 'You brought shame on your own head!'

His jaw tightened as if he was containing his anger. 'I'm sure we can be adult about this to the advantage of us both. You want the job, I want a chef who can cook food like my mother used to make,' he said quietly and suddenly it all made sense.

Misty grey eyes met melting brown. She saw his pain before he could conceal it and despite everything she felt a flood of sympathy for him. He knew that she'd learnt every one of his adored mother's recipes.

It occurred to her that she was his link with his mother, a potential recreation of those happy days when Sophia had poured all her heart and soul into cooking for her beloved son.

And then she realised he'd used the past tense. 'Used to? You mean…she's…dead?' she asked tentatively.

With a haunted expression he looked towards his desk. Although the large silver photo frame had its back to her, she knew it must be of Sophia because his eyes had misted over.

'Shortly after we arrived in Italy. Nine years, five months ago,' he said with touching precision. And added in a low growl, 'With her dying breath, she spoke of our dishonour and made me swear to—' His mouth clammed shut.

'Oh, Vido,' she said sadly.

That was the nub of his grief. He felt responsible for his mother's decline. His behaviour would have disappointed the fiercely upright and honest Sophia and she would have died full of regrets that her son had turned out so badly.

Yet inexplicably Anna felt deep sympathy for him. The anger and scorn had left his face. For a short moment he had become the man she remembered; an adoring and attentive son.

The thick black lashes lowered to hide the sadness in his eyes though it was still evident in his frown and in the tightness of his jaw and every line of his body. Staring at the ground, he muttered, 'I miss her, every day of my life.'

Her heart lurched. It had always touched her that he had loved his mother with such passion. He had been gentle and courteous towards Sophia, treating her as if she were a queen. Often Anna had found him cleaning the house or preparing the evening meal because his mother wasn't well. Yet he'd done it willingly because he'd adored her and saw it as his joy and duty to care for his sick mother.

Why Sophia had been so rude to her grandfather, she'd never know—only that it was obviously impossible for the proud old man to employ someone who'd insulted him. But she had missed Sophia, very much.

Wistfully Anna recalled how desperately she'd envied them the closeness of their relationship and the warm, demonstrative nature of their love. In the cramped, ugly little flat, she had glimpsed a family happiness that she'd wanted for herself.

Perhaps, she thought, that was what she'd hungered for. A small portion of Vido's affection. She hadn't loved *him* at all. Just the idea of being loved the way he loved his mother, totally and utterly.

'I'm sure you do. She was such a big part of your life and you were devoted to one another,' she said with understanding. 'I know you would have done anything for her. I can't tell you how sorry I am. I was very fond of her. And I admired her because she worked so hard—even when she wasn't feeling too good.'

He seemed incapable of speech, emotion chasing over his strained face. Her hand touched his arm, her fingers lightly resting on the silky shirt. In the back of her mind she was conscious of his warm skin beneath, and the steeliness of his flexing muscles as they tightened beneath her hand.

'Sophia was always kind to me,' she recalled, her eyes smoky with memories. 'Some of the happiest times I ever spent were when I was learning to cook in her kitchen.'

'I remember,' he husked. Silence hummed between them. 'Anna. Recreate that time,' he urged quietly. 'You'd have all the freedom in the world to cook whatever you like. All her recipes. I want that little bit of home.'

'I know,' she said, her heart melting at his longing.

Two-timer or not, fortune-hunter, a ruth-lessly ambitious man who'd stop at nothing to claw his way up the ladder to success, he had that one little bit of goodness in him. He had loved his mother. Perhaps he'd even embarked on that crooked route to the top because he'd wanted to care for his mother, to give her the best.

'Anna,' he said, his voice laden with fatal persuasion. 'I know this is a good job. You'd be mad to turn it down. You'd even have a share in the business, like everyone else. Some of my employees are wealthy in their own right.'

'Why on earth do they stay with you, then?' she queried in surprise.

'Ask them. They'll say they love the work. It's challenging and varied. But...' He gave one of his expressive shrugs. 'If you're not in-terested, if you're too proud to work here be-cause of an incident ten years ago between us, then that's up to you.'

As if dismissing her, he returned to his desk and began to collect together the papers there. She watched, her mind spinning. His dig about her pride had struck home. That was all that was stopping her. It oughtn't to come first. Her grandfather's well-being should be at the top of the list. A secure job and more money would make life so much better for him.

Pride shouldn't keep her from earning a decent salary. Why should it? If Vido's company was as democratic and as wonderful as he boasted, then she'd be a fool to walk away. He wouldn't want to jeopardise the ethos of his entire business by constantly sparring with her.

On the other hand, if he was lying and he was running something crooked, then she could fling a claim of misrepresentation at him and get out fast. She couldn't lose!

Her eyes sparkled with life. Even if she only lasted six months, it would get her out of a financial hole. She'd do it. Tell her grandfather that they were milking Vido for all they could get. That would go down well. She would swallow her pride and suffer Vido's triumph for her grandfather's sake.

But she wouldn't behave like a skivvy. She wasn't to be walked all over. He might learn that the hard way. Aware of the risk to her peace of mind that she was running in working for Vido, she took a deep breath, her hands clammy as common sense battled with practicalities.

She would. She wouldn't. She *must*.

'Is the kitchen still in the same place?'

He froze. Flicked his inky eyes at her and slowly placed the papers back on the desk. He'd got her. A surge of elation fired him up, demanding physical release. Short of flinging her down on the carpet then and there, and ravishing the living daylights out of her, he was forced to find another outlet.

She was engaged. Off limits. Something he must get into his brain so it could tell his libido. Which he hoped he could direct towards other women.

'I'll show you,' he said unnecessarily and strode out so quickly that he could hear her feet scurrying to catch up.

When she took one look at the old-fashioned kitchen she wrinkled her nose.

'I expected something wonderful,' she said with disappointment.

'It was due to be modernised last week,' he explained in haste, in case she was put off. 'The fitter broke his leg and we've been rescheduled by his team.'

'Poor man,' she said with surprising sympathy.

Her soft grey eyes scanned the untidy, uncared-for room she must know so well. Gradually he detected an easing of her stiffly held body. This place meant a lot to her. He filed that fact away in case it came in useful.

'It's a bit of a mess,' he conceded. 'The cleaner has only kept on top of the essential areas because of the planned revamp. It'll look better once it's had a good scrub.'

'No problem.' There was an air of excitement about her and the eagerness lit her face, stirring up emotions in his chest. 'You said... modernised.' She looked anxious.

'I'm not intending to go for stainless steel or wall-to-wall Formica,' he said drily. 'I was thinking of an unstructured look. The classic country kitchen. Free-standing pieces such as a large oak dresser and cupboards crafted from reclaimed timber, that kind of thing.' He saw her look of relief. 'My chef would have total control over the fittings,' he bribed.

She beamed as if he'd handed her the crown jewels. 'Thank goodness!' Her finger swept across the large pine table collecting a thin layer of dust. 'This needs attention before I start cooking—and all the surfaces and those mucky dishes.'

'I was supposed to do the dishes,' he explained. 'It's my turn today to tackle anything that doesn't fit in the dishwasher. I planned to leave everything till after the interviews—'

She wasn't listening. He watched her shed her jacket and hang it on the back of a chair. Then she lifted down one of the cleaner's overalls from its peg and kicked off her shoes.

'Are you intending to hang around here or do you have something better to do?' she demanded, her head high on her long, slender neck. Which he contemplated kissing. The skin was smooth and golden and seemed to be inviting his lips to— 'Vido? Did you hear me?'

He flashed a quick half-smile. No harm in looking, was there? Providing he didn't touch.

'Sorry. Miles away. I thought I'd watch you.'

She sniffed in disapproval as if he was some kind of pervert. Which, perhaps, he was. He couldn't keep his eyes off her. She'd become suddenly sure of herself, quick and light on her feet. His gaze dropped to them. They were small and with perfect arches—

'Turn around,' she commanded.

He blinked, bristling immediately. 'What—?'

'Turn around!'

Intrigued, he obeyed, little thrills fizzing through his nerves. He had no idea there were so many in his body, he marvelled.

But... Me Tarzan, you Jane, he thought. He was the boss. So why was she ordering him about? More than that, why was he letting her?

His acute hearing picked up the soft slither of stockings sliding over skin. His pulses took up a highly erratic beat. What was that? Her skirt?

Per l'amor di Dio! She was *stripping*?

'All right,' she said breathlessly.

All right? With his heart lurching about like crazy and curls of intense excitement boiling his loins? No, it wasn't all right. It was achingly delicious and uncomfortable. *Dio!* He wanted her more than he'd ever wanted anyone in the whole of his life. And she was unavailable.

Taking a deep breath, he turned around, pretending to lounge casually against the fridge in the hope that it might cool him down.

His disappointment was acute. His excitement crashed down to subterranean levels. There she was, briskly demure and half-swamped in the large overall, efficiently stacking dishes while the hot tap filled the vast butler sink.

On the chair he could see her skirt and stockings. His eyes widened and flicked back to her. As she reached for the large oval plate, which had held the assortment of bacon, sausages and eggs for breakfast, the overall obligingly parted to allow him a glimpse of tanned thigh. His breathing became fractured.

'I'll soak these dishes that I can't fit in the dishwasher,' she said, oblivious to his salacious thoughts, 'then you can show me what food stores there are. While I'm scrubbing the table I can decide what to cook. Right.' She dropped the silver cutlery into a jar of hot water and pushed the last pan into the suds before wiping her hands on a towel. 'What do we have?'

Before he could answer, there was a call from the hallway.

'Veee-do-o-o! Oh! There you are. I've been looking for you everywhere.' Camilla paused in the doorway, shooting a quick glance at Anna. The two women looked at one another like wary dogs poised to fight. 'Your new chef?' Camilla's eyebrows arched high into her aristocratic forehead.

'Depends,' he muttered with studied nonchalance that didn't quite convince him, let alone the perceptive Camilla. 'What is it?'

'Milan. They need a decision—'

'Then make it.'

Her eyebrows went even higher at his abruptness. 'I hear and obey. You take care,' she warned, before turning on her Laurenti heels and sweeping out.

'Coffee?' he suggested to Anna, needing an activity to relieve his tension. Camilla had effortlessly identified his obsession. He hoped it wasn't that obvious to Anna herself.

'First show me the store cupboard. It's not where it used to be,' she said firmly, shutting the old larder door.

'It wasn't large enough for my needs.' He strode over to the old dairy, knowing she'd be impressed. 'There,' he said, only just managing to suppress a childish desire to cry, Tarra!

'Oh!' Her face shone with awe. 'It's wonderful!' She went inside. 'Borlotti!' she muttered to herself. 'And sacks of rice and chickpeas—and 00 grade durum. Perfect. Sea salt, extra-virgin cold-pressed olive oil, Parmesan in muslin, olives, anchovy paste, capers, almonds, vanilla pods, pasta...' Her fingers caressed the dried goods as though they were her lovers. He smiled to himself, amused that he should envy a stack of groceries. Then she saw the dried meats hanging on hooks from the ceiling. 'Fantastic! Prosciutti, salami, a whole ham and proper sausages—Vido, I have to admit, it's a chef's paradise,' she declared, her flushed face turning to his.

She was enchanting. Gone was the stilted, prim woman whose cold manner could have chilled Africa and given it Arctic frosts for a month. She had become someone entirely different. Alive and passionate.

At that moment he wanted her very badly.

Before he knew it, his finger had lifted to flick away a bubble of soapsuds from her cheek. She gasped, presumably at his temerity, but he thought she might also have felt the spark that had leapt between them. It had certainly seared him with its intensity.

'Soap,' he explained unnecessarily.

'Oh.'

She seemed incapable of moving. Her enormous velvet-grey eyes looked up at him and he felt as if his brain had gone swimming. Afraid he might jump her and ruin his plans for a slow and increasingly wild seduction, he crushed his longing to kiss that petal-soft mouth and zapped a frown onto his face.

'You'd better inspect the fridge.'

She flushed. 'Of course.'

She seemed nervous as she examined the contents of the American-sized refrigerator, but grew more and more sure of herself, obviously noting the supplies with a practised eye.

'The freezer.' He opened the massive door, proud of the goods he'd imported. Her reaction was more than pleasing.

'This is heaven,' she muttered to herself.

'Is it?' he murmured, recklessly close to her glowing body.

But she had eyes only for the frozen pancetta she was turning over in her hands with all the rapt attention of a mother tending her baby. With obvious reluctance she replaced the pancetta and shut the freezer door.

She felt almost delirious with delight. The store cupboard could have fed an army for a year. The freezer could have housed an entire herd of cattle. The fridge contained everything she could have wanted in her kitchen— and more.

In a dream, she turned to Vido and found herself just a few heat-inducing inches from his broad chest. For the life of her, she didn't know what she'd intended to say. So out came the truth.

'I really do want to work here,' she confessed breathily to his waistcoat buttons.

'You'd better start cooking, then,' he suggested, the buttons heaving about oddly.

Puzzled, she darted a quick glance at him from under her fringe of black lashes. Mistake. For a moment, she felt herself swaying closer, mesmerised by the awesome nature of his sexual attraction. It was like a living thing, playing with her, reeling her in. And she knew why women had succumbed to him. There was something about him that appealed to her raw physical needs, promising the best sex ever.

The darkness of his eyes intensified, pulling her closer. His carnal mouth seemed soft and hungry and she imagined his pearly teeth sinking into her parted lips, gently tugging...

The touch of his fingers on her forearm brought her crashing back to reality. 'What will you give me, Anna?'

Blinking, she looked down to where his forefinger was absently moving over her tingling flesh. Just a millionth of an inch. It was enough.

'Give?' she croaked, visions of them both entwined in a naked celebration of liberated lovemaking.

'To eat,' he said softly, his eyes suggesting something quite different.

Moving back so that his infuriatingly erotic caress couldn't continue a second longer, she tried to get a hold of herself.

'I thought—' Curses. Her breathing was letting her down. Digging her nails into her palms, she felt her brain suddenly clear of the fog that had descended. 'A simple pasta dish to start with,' she said in a rush. 'Say...a pasta roulade, filled with spinach and ricotta and herbs. Then that side of lamb stuffed with rosemary, and—and chestnut cake to finish.'

'*Castagnaccio,*' he purred, rolling the word around his tongue and making it sound like a lover's compliment. 'I haven't had that since...' He slammed his mouth shut. It was a moment before he continued and his voice was unbearably husky with emotion. Her heart went out to him because she knew he was remembering the last time his mother had cooked the cake for him. 'I can't wait.' He gave her a faint smile. 'I think that tonight we will go to bed satisfied.'

She was suffocating. Smothered by essence of man. And thinking darkly that she wouldn't feel satisfied at all.

'You'll end up with a boiled egg if you don't get out of my way,' she muttered, pulling things—any things—out of the fridge. 'Off you go so I can get on.'

'You know,' he mused in an unnervingly slow and liquefying voice that opened her body up to him, 'there are only two activities that use all the senses.' Like an idiot she paused, waiting wide-eyed for him to continue, her breath deserting her lungs. 'One is making love. The other is cooking,' he murmured, the gleam in his eyes telling her that he was a devotee of both.

'I'll stick with the second of those,' she said jerkily, pushing past him. Her starved lungs inhaled the scent of him and her nerve-endings twitched excruciatingly. So her voice was tart and irritable when she flung back, 'Making love is not on my agenda.'

Though she wished it were. She had to do something to satisfy her demented hunger. Perhaps it was like a biological clock, she thought gloomily. Her body was beginning to protest that she'd starved it.

'Poor fiancé. He must be very frustrated,' he mocked.

Not half as frustrated as she was. 'Where's that coffee?' she snapped, with scant regard for their relative positions.

Vido waited for his pulses to stop running a marathon and thought of her intriguing remark about sex. Could that explain the hunger that poured out of her and set him on fire? More to the point, could she be still a virgin? It would explain the air of innocence that mingled with her natural sexiness, and which made her blush every time he made a questionable comment.

The marathon began again. His heartbeat racked up a notch or two and he did his best to tame his galloping blood pressure by vigorously wiping over the marble-topped table he'd had imported from Milan.

'I got this table specially, for working pasta,' he said unnecessarily when he'd finished.

Bent over the sack of flour, Anna ignored him and continued to fill a bowl with it, perfectly aware that he was now admiring her back view.

'Black,' she prompted icily, seeing that he'd only got as far as standing by the gleaming new espresso machine. 'One sugar.'

And she stalked back to gather the ingredients she needed. Free-range organic eggs. Sea salt. Extra-virgin cold-pressed olive oil. Her tension evaporated like magic as she sifted the flour onto the marble slab. It fell like a fine cloud and formed into the shape of a volcano.

Lovingly her small fist made a well in the centre. Her face became free of anxiety, all her concentration focused on the pleasure ahead.

He hungered for the fluidity of her body and had to discipline himself severely to stay by the hissing, snorting machine. Every languorous, loving movement she made mesmerised him.

Reverently she cracked the eggs, her lush mouth parted with pleasure as she added the salt. Her hands plunged into the mixture, combining the ingredients until they became a sticky paste. Back and forth. Back and forth. Vido's loins tightened.

Panting softly, her small white teeth visible against the darkness of her mouth, she began to knead, the rhythm of her body and the arch of her back quite beautiful to watch. A warm liquidity flowed through him. Never in his life had he ever known anything so exquisitely arousing.

Surreptitiously he put on a CD and Pavarotti's passionate arias filled the room. Anna smiled to herself and her graceful arms seemed to move in perfect time with the music.

He felt overwhelmed by powerful emotions, which all seemed to be bound up in the small figure of the woman lyrically swaying backwards and forwards as she kneaded the dough.

Surrendering to his senses, he watched the dough become elastic, springing eagerly beneath her practised hands as if it were a living thing. Which, on reflection, he supposed it was. A serene joy seemed to surround her and it affected him deeply as her passion communicated itself to him.

Her movements, the perfect curve of her jaw and the sweet arcs of her arms, were unutterably sensual. Strands of curling ebony hair were escaping from her prim little chignon with the vigour of her attack on the dough and they were drifting down to frame her face with an appealing abandon.

Absently her hands kept pushing her hair back into place, leaving those appealing little daubs of flour everywhere, which he'd remembered from the past.

Irresistible. And he hated her for causing his arousal. Hated her more fiercely than ever because he wanted to be consumed by the kind of woman who'd become his wife. Not the granddaughter of the man who might have been the root cause of his mother's death. Not the spiteful hellcat of a woman who'd blackened his name without a moment's thought.

But his brain seemed to have lost its connection with his body. He found himself standing behind her before he realised he'd moved. Close to, he could see every detail of the soft, achingly vulnerable nape of her neck and the fineness of the tendrils of glassy black hair. Her shoulders were slight, her back lithe and straining with effort, the long corded muscles beside her spine demanding his caress.

After a moment her movements slowed. She knew he was there. He held his breath, waiting.

As if unable to stand it any longer, she turned, clearly as shocked as he was by the bolt of electricity that crackled between them.

'What...?'

There was flour in tempting little smudges all over her face just waiting to be brushed away by his questing fingers. To be followed by his mouth. Tongue. Teeth. Hell. He wanted to ravage her, to subdue her till she begged for mercy.

Like him, she was breathing heavily. Her spine had been thrust back against the table and she couldn't move away, a situation he found unbearably tempting and erotic.

He could kiss her now and she wouldn't resist. Hazily he realised that she had been partially aroused by her love of cooking. If she ever responded to him he wanted it to be for him, and him alone. Not as a side effect of making pasta, he thought angrily.

'Did you say one sugar?' he clipped, to kill his lust stone dead.

She jerked as if he'd hit her and turned abruptly back, smashing her fist into the dough.

'Yes,' she growled, pummelling with impressive ferocity.

Muttering oaths under his breath, he stalked off, hampered somewhat by his own arousal. That had been stupid in the extreme. He had to remember that she was engaged. He was supposed to be an honourable man—though his feelings were far from that at the moment. Every instinct was screaming at him to take her, then and there. Then to send her away, free at last of the terrible shackles she'd clamped on him.

Unfortunately, seducing her wasn't compatible with his avowed honour. Any attempt to get her into his bed would confirm that her assessment of his character had been correct.

Dio! How could he prove himself to be honourable *and* satisfy his catastrophic physical need for her?

'Coffee.'

Controlling his breathing, he slid it onto the table where she was brushing the dough with oil then covering it with a damp cloth so that it could rest. His testosterone levels needed a rest too. Perhaps, he thought ruefully, watching her convey it to the fridge, he should slide onto the shelf with the damn pasta and cool down.

'Thank you.'

The ache was beginning to gnaw at him intolerably. Pretending nonchalance, he lounged against the worktop and nibbled an amoretto biscuit, wondering what the hell he was going to do.

Pink-faced from effort—he assumed—Anna briskly washed her hands and proceeded to chop rosemary and garlic, which she stuffed into the side of lamb. With great care, her small pink tongue sticking out as she did so, and making his insides melt, she neatly sewed up the lamb and put it in a tin before pouring on white wine and slipping the dish into the roasting oven.

The aromas of his boyhood were tantalising his senses. His head was swimming. Perhaps he needed a cold douche. And what better, he suddenly realised, than to see Anna playing footsie with her fiancé and gazing adoringly into the man's eyes?

'I hope you don't find it too intimidating meeting everyone tonight,' he said, injecting as much doubt into his tone as he could.

Her eyes flashed to his in immediate concern. 'Why? Should I?' she asked warily.

Her nervousness was obvious. She'd oiled the cake tin twice.

'Possibly. We can be a pretty high-powered lot. I am rather throwing you to the lions and you'd be the centre of attention because they'd all be assessing you,' he said, laying it on with a trowel. 'Why don't you invite someone you know to give you moral support?' he asked with what he hoped was deceptive innocence.

Ever since she was seventeen, she'd tried to build up her self-assurance. But Vido knew her of old, and he was right. The evening daunted her because it was vital that she succeeded. For her grandpa's sake, for Peter's, for her own pride and financial stability.

She thought of her various friends who might come, and then she beamed. There was one ideal person to accompany her. Not only was he used to swimming with the sharks in the world of business, but his presence would offer protection of a kind.

Tensely he watched, willing her to choose her boyfriend.

'How about my fiancé?' she asked, with a rush of eager excitement that illogically annoyed him. 'He's in London, but he'd be thrilled to come over.'

He produced an 'if-you-must' shrug and paid a good deal of attention to stirring his espresso to disguise his satisfaction. He badly needed to see them together. It might be an evening of masochism for him, but at least it would kill his desire for Anna if he realised that she was committed, body and soul, to this city slicker.

'Fine. He can stay here tonight if you like.' He hesitated, struck by the obvious. She might want to sleep with her fiancé. He clenched his teeth together hard. Thinking of Anna sighing with delight in another man's arms was ridiculously uncomfortable to contemplate. With an effort, he bit the bullet and offered her up on a plate to her fiancé. 'Unless...' He held his breath, meeting her eyes then with an intensely watchful stare. Virgin or not? Suddenly it seemed to have become a matter of great importance to him. 'Unless you want him to go back to your house.'

Anna tensed and immediately busied herself with weighing the chestnut flour.

'Two-fifty...three hundred grams,' she muttered, wondering why the thought of making love with Peter should be so distasteful to her when she would have leapt into Vido's bed with alacrity if there could have been no consequences whatsoever. 'I'm sure Peter would be delighted to accept your invitation for dinner. He's very interested in Solutions Inc. Since he'd need to leave early in the morning, it would make more sense if he stayed here tonight, thank you,' she said coolly.

He didn't comment straight away and when she shot him a puzzled glance she saw that he was pushing his hands through his hair and looking rather distracted. Shaken, even. Seeing him so dishevelled and vulnerable made her heart lurch.

It struck her that she was still searching for love—and stupidly imagining that Vido could provide it merely because she found him sexually exciting. The two didn't necessarily go together, of course.

But it occurred to her that she wasn't sure if love or sex figured in her relationship with Peter at all. In fact it had worried her that he'd been finding excuses not to visit, ever since it had become public knowledge that her grandfather had sold his factory and Stanford House and she was no longer an heiress.

Doubts filled her mind. Initially Peter had been wonderfully attentive. A perfect gentleman. But lately he'd been rather curt with her. She'd put that down to the stress of his job. It could be that in the beginning, Peter had latched on to her because of her financial prospects. She felt slightly sick. And knew she must seriously examine her own feelings for him that very night.

'Your fiancé is welcome.' Vido's voice was unmistakably shaky.

'Are you all right?' she asked with a puzzled frown.

He gave a secretive smile. 'I could be. Ask me tomorrow.'

'I don't understand.' She couldn't look away. Felt as if she was on shifting sand.

'You will. Call your fiancé. Invite him.'

A strange excitement seemed to be simmering inside him. He smiled as he held out his mobile to her.

She didn't want to go over to him. The space between them was already thick with tension and narrowing the gap would crush the air out of her.

He seemed to understand this because he put the phone down on the worktop and moved to the French doors to study the giant cedar spreading its branches across the billiard-table lawn.

Horribly agitated, she hurried to the phone. Maybe hearing Peter's voice would put her emotions back on course.

'Talbot.'

Nothing. She felt nothing at all. No lift of her heart or her spirits. No fireworks going off in her head, as they did when she looked at Vido. Appalled by the implications of that, she ventured a subdued, 'It's me.'

'Doesn't sound like good news,' he said with undisguised disappointment. 'Oh, Anna! What did you do wrong? I can't believe you've blown it,' he complained irritably. 'You're hopeless. We'd worked out a great interviewee technique—'

She hardly heard Peter's petulant reproach. Her huge grey eyes were fixed on Vido again, homing in on him as if he was the centre of her life. Slowly he turned and the involuntary clenching of her body flung her mind into turmoil.

He was scrutinising her in a very odd way. She realised that he must be puzzled that she and Peter didn't coo at one another. But she wasn't lovey-dovey. Never had been.

She broke in on Peter's censure, annoyed at his assumption. 'You've got it all wrong.' She tried to kill the irritation. Vido's eyebrows had lifted in surprise at her tone so she injected sweetness and light into it. 'I'm on trial. Darling.' The endearment was squeezed out after a brief hesitation and sounded odd even to her ears. 'I'm cooking dinner and you've been invited along. It would be wonderful if you could come,' she added, trying to believe that herself. 'You can stay the night at Stanford House,' she finished stiltedly, in case Peter got the wrong idea.

Tension seemed to be holding Vido unnaturally still. He knew she wasn't starry-eyed about Peter, she thought, her throat drying. She licked her lips and shuddered at the slow, predatory smile that curved his hungry mouth.

Peter had to come, she thought frantically. If only to protect her from her chaotic hormones and Vido's casual attitude to sex. If Vido ever realised how she felt, he'd be sliding her into his bed before she knew it—just for the hell of it. Another notch on his bedpost.

A golden, liquid warmth melted her entire body, prompting her to think 'so what?'.

Outrageous! She despaired of herself.

Suddenly she realised that Peter was already accepting and she forced herself to concentrate on what he was saying.

'...fantastic! I never thought you'd do it!' Peter enthused.

'I'm not there yet,' she cautioned. 'It depends on the meal and whether I get on with the rest of the staff—'

He wasn't listening. '...everything I'd hoped for. I can use the opportunity to make myself known! I'll tell them about myself and ask to be considered for a job. Great stuff. I'll leave now so I can get in as much networking as possible. See you later. Don't be surprised if I don't spend much time with you. There's a lot at stake here for me.'

He'd cut the connection. Dreading his arrival now and alarmed that Solutions Inc might take him on, she wondered how on earth she'd get through the evening. Vido would expect her to show affection towards Peter. The way she was feeling now, she'd barely be able to give him the time of day.

Feeling distinctly edgy, she softened her face in the hope that her voice would be warm and loving as a result, and said into the totally empty ether, 'Bye, darling. Look forward to that.'

Vido had moved close to her again. With her eyes fixed in a cowardly gaze at his midriff, she held out the phone. His hand closed over hers and she looked up at him as her pulses fluttered as if a thousand butterflies were trapped in her body.

'When did you say you're marrying him?' Vido asked softly.

Panic ripped through her. There couldn't be a marriage. It would be a travesty to marry a man she didn't love. Her mouth opened but no sound came out. Eventually she fudged, 'I said two months. Why?'

He had to stop her from making a terrible mistake. She had no real, deep feelings for the man. She just needed to be loved.

If he kissed her now he knew she'd respond. It might even prove to her that this Peter wasn't the man for her. Vido gave a silent groan. The trouble was, he was hamstrung by honour.

The ache in his body had become even more intolerable.

'Why?' He thought rapidly. 'Well, holiday arrangements would be necessary if we took you on,' he explained. Frowning, he checked his watch. 'I've been here long enough. I have a date with a horse,' he muttered. 'See you at seven-thirty.'

'Wait!' she breathed.

He paused, almost shaking in his efforts to stay away from her. When he wanted to pull her roughly towards him, envelop her in his arms and kiss her until she moaned for more.

'What?' he snapped.

'I—I was w-wondering,' she stumbled, and stopped as if she was apprehensive.

His wretched protective gene asserted itself and made him relax his brusque manner. Looking down on her upturned, anxious face, those grey eyes wide and soulful and the trembling mouth alluringly petal-soft, he felt a lurch of recklessness come over him. She was willing. He knew that. Perhaps...

His eyes darkened as he melted. 'Yes?' he husked encouragingly, letting the word linger on his mouth.

'What—?'

Anna blinked, evidently surprised by the squeak that had emerged from her throat. His gaze went there. To the long, slender perfection of it. He would dip his tongue into that little hollow where her pulse leapt so tellingly...

'What shall I wear?' she whispered.

Shaken from his contemplation of her slender jawline and his calculation of how many kisses it would take to reach her ear, he wondered if he'd heard correctly.

'Wear.' And she nodded. His breath shuddered out. So that had been the reason for her anxiety! And he, like a fool, had imagined that she was as affected by their closeness as he was. 'People wear what they like.' The voice that had emerged didn't sound like his own. More like a rasping saw cutting through steel. Anna had backed away, assuming that he was annoyed by her all-too-feminine worries. 'Camilla usually puts on something long and glamorous. Some of the other women wear jeans, like a few of the men. Anyone with Italian blood tends to opt for understated, classic casuals. No rules. Wear whatever you like.'

Before he could react to her crushed and subdued appearance, he headed for the door for a long and ice-cold shower to be followed by a furious gallop across the fields on his favourite Arab stallion.

He scowled his way across the hall. Anna had got to him. And how. It was supposed to be the other way round. Maybe he'd do better to send her packing. For once in his life, he didn't know what to do. He needed a troubleshooter, he thought grimly.

'Vido! I want a moment of your time,' called Camilla, hurrying up to him with a sheaf of papers.

'Not *now*!' he barked, his voice echoing across the vast space. Almost immediately he felt ashamed and shot out an arm to stop her from turning away. 'I'm sorry,' he apologised. 'Bad temper. Forgive me.'

She gave him a smile of friendly understanding. 'She really bugs you, doesn't she?' Her cool hand rested on his beating heart and she looked up at his face with sympathy. 'Listen to that!' she scolded. 'And now you listen to some advice from someone who cares about you. Kiss her, yell at her, seduce her or put the fear of God into her, but don't let her go until you've sorted things out between you,' she advised. 'Or you'll forever be unsettled—and abominably rude and scratchy to your adoring staff!' she scolded.

Tenderly he gazed down on her, his hands resting on her shoulders. She was right. As always.

'You are a woman in a million. Some man's going to be very lucky, one day.'

'Yes,' she said serenely. 'Though that man isn't you any more.'

He laughed in acknowledgement and tweaked her nose. 'I adore you,' he said, feeling more cheerful. And as she walked away smiling, he called teasingly, affectionately, after her, '*Adore* you, Camilla, woman in a million!' and she gave a little wave of her hand in regal acknowledgement.

Frozen with shock in the shadows, Anna stared as Vido ran up the stairs. She had been right. Vido and Camilla were lovers. When she'd run to the kitchen door that led into the hall, prompted by Vido's angry roar, she hadn't expected to witness the closeness between him and Camilla. But although she hadn't been able to hear everything they'd said—except for his last remark—the tender affection between them had been unmistakable.

She scowled. That made Vido's sexual interest in *her* even more reprehensible. She might have known that his knee-jerk flirting had been his normal reaction to any reasonable-looking woman. He was a lecher and came on strong as naturally as breathing. She winced.

And knew it was time she faced up to the awful truth. Crazy though it seemed, she had wanted Vido to adore her. To fall madly in love with her and fill her hollow heart with passion. Yet she knew perfectly well that he was materialistic, selfish, and used people without compunction—especially women.

She groaned, hating the fact that such a louse could possess her hungry mind and body so easily. She was a hostage to her own emotions. If only, she thought sickly, she knew how to break free!

CHAPTER FIVE

SHE had twenty minutes to dash home—which fortunately was not far—whip her clothes off, shower and fling something on for the evening. Any old thing. Like her frumpy, sack-like dress…

Every brain cell she possessed leapt into rebellion, demanding insistently that she should conjure up something sensational from her wardrobe. Racing down the driveway, she rebuked herself for being so vain.

Sensational? If only! She'd never look as good as the elegant Italian women or the stunning Camilla. There was nothing on her coat hangers that could be considered even remotely eye-catching.

She grimaced. So what? But not the sack. She had her pride. It would have to be her long, raspberry-red skirt and a demure top, then.

Fifteen minutes later, she was perversely discarding the horribly ladylike sleeveless shirt she usually wore with the skirt and rummaging around for something more exotic. Or did she mean erotic?

And why, she asked herself, her fingers closing on something she dared not—should not—wear, was she so darn determined to knock 'em dead tonight? It wasn't only because she wanted to make a good impression with her cooking. She wanted to be liked—and accepted—by Vido's staff.

As for Vido himself... No. She really wouldn't even go there. Before she could examine her motives too closely, she dragged on the tight-fitting top she'd unearthed and faced herself in the mirror.

'Wow!' she whispered.

OK, her face was flushed from rushing around like a headless chicken and her eyes were sparkling for the same reason, but the top certainly had that wow factor even if it had been a mad purchase at the local charity shop.

A fabulous tangerine, its sheer quality stopped it from screaming at the red skirt. The bootlace straps drew the eye down to the beautiful cut of the bodice, which sat snugly around her untrammelled breasts and pushed them into faintly discernible mounds below the scooped neckline.

With her sheet of black hair streaming down over her shoulders, the entire outfit made her feel fantastic. It slithered beautifully over her body in a highly sensual way, caressing her skin with the delicacy of a lover.

She frowned at the line of her briefs showing through the fine fabric of the skirt. It hadn't bothered her before but she knew that the Italians in the party would mark her down for such a fashion *faux pas*.

Hesitating at the enormity of what she should do, she eventually bowed to the need to look as perfect as possible and removed the offending knickers.

She gulped. The sensation of silk against her naked buttocks made her feel quite abandoned. But the effect was worth it. She looked great, that was the main thing. And no one would know she wasn't wearing any underwear.

'I am confident. I can do this. I will succeed,' she said to herself, actually believing that she could.

Slipping on a pair of high-heeled sandals without a thought for the work that she had ahead of her in the kitchen, she pushed on her engagement ring, grabbed her butcher's apron, slammed the door behind her and headed for Stanford House again.

Once there, she hastily checked the lamb. It had been left to rest in the simmer oven with the little gem lettuces which she'd stuffed with pine nuts, sultanas, anchovies, capers and black olives. Perfect.

With her stomach swooping as if she was hurtling up and down a lift shaft in a fifty-storey building, she slid out the tray of nibbles she'd prepared earlier and put the canapés on two plates. Then she straightened her back, lifted her chin and strode towards the drawing room and the sound of voices as though she hadn't a care in the world.

Afflicted by nerves however, she paused in the doorway, arrested by the sight that greeted her eyes. The room looked wonderful, like a scene in a film. It glowed warmly in the light of huge candles and low table lamps shed golden pools of light in strategic places. Adding to the effect, a crackling log fire burned in the great stone fireplace to take off the slight chill of the evening.

The room seemed to be filled with glamorous-looking people, many of them straight out of the pages of a fashion magazine.

Confidently they lounged on the sofas or stood in unaffectedly elegant attitudes, chatting animatedly. There was a tangible atmosphere of ease, the kind of relaxation only achieved by people who were completely comfortable with one another.

Feeling a total outsider, she hesitated to go in, afflicted by a sudden dose of cold feet. Her wide, grey-eyed gaze had settled on Vido, who was listening in amusement to something Camilla was saying. And the spear of involuntary jealousy that struck her made Anna draw in her breath sharply just as Vido noticed her, the smile wiped from his face in an instant.

She jerked her head away and pretended that she was looking for Peter. Perhaps Vido was worried she might tell Camilla that he'd been flirting, she thought with contempt.

'Anna!' To her surprise, Camilla had broken away from Vido and the two men who'd been hanging on her every word, and was hurrying forward to meet her. 'I'm Camilla. Vido's PA. Hi. You look...fantastic,' she said politely. 'Love the top.'

'Charity shop, one pound twenty. It's probably thrilled to be somewhere decent for a change,' Anna stumbled.

Camilla giggled and thawed noticeably. 'Just say thank you! I don't want a pedigree!'

'Nerves,' Anna confessed, immediately liking the woman, quite against all her expectations. 'I'm terrified.'

'Nobody's going to bite you,' Camilla said, amused.

Vido might, Anna thought. She sighed. 'You all look so confident. It's like being in front of the class again, reading out an essay with everyone's eyes glued on me.'

Perhaps something in her tone had indicated that her schooldays had been a torment. Or maybe Vido had told Camilla that Anna's nose had once given her the appearance of a witch in *Macbeth*. Whatever the reason, the woman's expression softened and she put a friendly hand on Anna's shoulder.

'You're not what I expected,' Camilla said frankly.

'Thanks, Vido.' She wrinkled her nose. 'He gave the impression my character might be close to that of Godzilla and Lucrezia Borgia?' she hazarded.

Camilla laughed a little uncomfortably. 'Something like that.'

'Well, it's not. I told him a few home truths about himself when we were teenagers and he's never forgiven me. He went off the rails when his mother lost her job and I found his behaviour impossible. But I've done nothing to be ashamed of, I swear. He's got me all wrong,' she insisted, desperate to be believed. She wouldn't have a chance if Vido's twisted views prevailed.

For several seconds, Camilla studied Anna's open, anxious face. 'Hmm. Maybe he has. None so blind, eh? He's normally very perceptive. How odd. How *interesting*. I must say, Steve reckoned you'd fit in well. He liked you immediately. Well, take it from me, whatever trouble there was between you and Vido in the past, we're all rooting for you, Godzilla or not—so long as you don't do a Lucrezia and poison us!' she said with a wonderfully warm smile. 'Vido is desperate for a chef who can cook decent Italian food and we're fed up with him telling us what wonderful dishes his *mama* used to make. And staying with the theme of dodgy characters from history, I do believe that he'd consider taking on Atilla the Hun if he could do a cracking spag bol.'

Things were looking up. With Camilla on her side, the job might be hers.

'I could grow a beard and get a helmet,' Anna offered with a smile.

Camilla giggled again. 'And ruin that fab face?' she said in mock horror. 'Now. Hang on to your hat. Everyone!' She clapped her hands, gaining instant attention. 'Darlings, this is Anna Willoughby,' she announced. 'She's cooking for us tonight and—if we're very nice to her and beg her on bended knee—she'll dish up a meal every night thereafter till she's sick of the sight of us.'

Vido was glad that his staff had moved *en bloc* to greet her. It gave him precious moments to recover from Anna's startling entrance.

Only Camilla's quick thinking had diverted Joe and his lawyer from teasing him about the way his jaw had slowly dropped open at the sight of the siren who'd appeared in the doorway.

Anna looked utterly edible. His fertile mind fed on this. In his imagination he saw her naked on a table surrounded by delicacies she had cooked. And he was nibbling and licking her from head...

'Canapé?'

Avoiding Anna's frosty eyes, he looked at the plate in a daze and lifted something green from the plate she was offering. Thinking of her, he bit into it gently. His taste buds rioted and for a brief moment his eyes closed of their own volition.

He could hear her breathing step up a pace. It matched his. Short, fast, hard. And hot.

'That's as-asparagus tips on tapenade on toast,' she informed him croakily, not bothering to describe the rest.

Some comment seemed necessary. 'I didn't expect this,' he muttered to the plate, his palate clamouring for more. So was every male cell in his body. She cooked like an angel. Looked like a siren. Every man's dream.

Camilla's face came close to his and she whispered, 'There's a lot you didn't expect, Vido, darling!'

He frowned, and when he looked up Anna had gone, to be engulfed in a horde of hungry men—though whether they were after her canapés or a leisurely glimpse of her incredible figure in that unnervingly slinky outfit, he didn't like to think.

Except that he wanted to drag them all away with a roar of possession and carry her up to his lair. Slide his hands over the silk that covered her. Slip it up to expose the warm satin skin...

He scowled, furious that she should have total sway over his masculinity. And he felt irritated by his raging lust. Dammit, he was no better than an animal. All he had in his head was Anna. Crazy thoughts of making love to her. The scowl deepened.

'I don't think I ought to take her on,' he told Camilla thickly, torn between his business sense and his need to see her hour by hour, every day, and to spend every night with her until he was rid of his madness.

'You'd be stupid to reject her. These canapés are out of this world.' Camilla munched happily. 'I went in the kitchen a while ago and drooled at the delights she's got waiting in the simmer oven. I think,' she said with a wicked grin, 'there are other delights waiting on simmer and they're all for you.'

'What do you mean?' he growled irritably.

'You know perfectly well. She's dazzled by you.'

'Rubbish. She's engaged.'

His heart did a little bump. But she was not in love. So the coast was clear...

'That relationship must be a mistake,' Camilla dismissed, reinforcing the opinion he'd formed earlier. 'Or sparks wouldn't be flying between the two of you. Stop pussy-footing around and declare your interest before you explode.'

Resisting an eager impulse to do just what his PA had suggested, he shook his head.

'She loathes me and I loathe her.'

'In a very sexual way,' Camilla murmured.

He drew in a sharp breath. Tried to be sensible. 'Nothing much passes by you, does it? But I have to think of the staff—'

She laughed and patted his face affectionately. 'We'll decide what we think of her. She's not at all the kind of person you described.'

'You're not usually fooled,' he reproved.

'No. And you're usually a good judge of character.'

His scowl returned. 'I've told you about her. What she did.'

'Yes. It doesn't tally with the person I see, though. I think you've got your wires crossed—or someone's crossed them for you. Look, Vido. Observe. It's what you're good at.'

His eyes flicked over to where Anna was talking to Joe and back again. 'She knows she's on show,' he grumped. 'It's in her interests to suck up to everyone.'

'I don't see it like that. What about the small, telling gestures? The body language? You're more of an expert than I am, and even I can tell that she's unsure of herself, unworldly and not snobbish at all. And look at that innocent face! There isn't a spiteful bone in her body. I'd stake my reputation on the fact that she's honest as the day is long and you've made a terrible mistake about her.'

'Are you mad?' He realised that his PA wasn't always right in assessing people.

'No, I'm just not burdened with your baggage,' Camilla said coolly. 'Personally, I'd say she'd fit in very well. Look at her.'

'I'm trying not to.'

'Slight trouble in the trousers department?' she asked.

Vido had to laugh. 'Understatement.'

But he looked to where Anna stood and knew that now the problem of Peter had been cleared up, he would do everything in his power to be her lover before the night was over. A feeling of exhilaration lifted his heart. To say nothing of everything south of his belt.

Anna's eyes slanted to his. It felt as if she'd plugged him into the mains.

'Sparks,' Camilla murmured.

'You're brilliant,' he murmured, his eyes alight with hungry fires. And he gave her a little hug.

Surreptitiously, Anna watched the exchange between the two of them.

'They're close, aren't they?' she said to Vido's immaculately suited gardener, Joe, hoping she sounded casually interested.

'Like *that*.' Joe curled his middle finger around his forefinger. 'She's gorgeous, don't you think?' They both looked at Camilla admiringly then Joe sighed as if in pleasure. 'They've been together for years.'

'Oh.' Again the awful jealousy.

'We're a pretty tight-knit community. I really hope you'll join us.'

'Thank you,' she said with a grateful smile.

She hadn't expected to be accepted with such enthusiasm. Her eyes sparkled with relief. Even if Vido was surly and difficult, she could stick out the six months with the friendship of these lovely people.

'Glass of wine?' Joe smiled at her in query.

'Better not. I can't start drinking now!' she protested with a laugh. 'I must go and cook the pasta—'

'Nonsense,' he said firmly. He poured her a glass. 'We have to make you properly welcome. Dinner can wait. Vido won't mind. Drink up while we all check you over.'

She smiled and capitulated, won over by his non-threatening manner. 'You *have* made me welcome,' she said, sipping the delicate white wine. 'I was so scared of meeting you all—'

'No monsters here, just pussy cats—even Vido!' laughed a striking Italian woman who had just drifted to Anna's side. 'I'm Condalita. Welcome. Be nice to me if you want sacks of fagioli. I hold the purse strings around here.'

'She means she's the accountant. Brainy and beautiful. Is life fair?' A freckled redhead, her hair twisted into extraordinary spikes, exchanged an easy grin with Condalita then shook Anna's hand. 'Lucy. I do the cleaning,'

Lucy announced. 'Everyone is great, honest. No bitching, no prima donnas. It's like being in a big family—but without the rows.'

Anna laughed with the others and was just getting over the sight of Lucy's psychedelic T-shirt and tight leather trousers when she saw Steve ushering Peter into the room. Dark and striking, dressed conventionally in a dark charcoal suit, fine striped shirt and co-ordinating tie, nevertheless her fiancé seemed suddenly blank and charmless.

Her eyes flicked over to Vido and she made an instant comparison. His moleskin trousers clung to his narrow hips, the pale caramel colour echoing that of his soft shirt. Without making any effort, he commanded the entire room by sheer force of personality alone.

It wasn't just his good looks that drew her to him—Peter was technically just as handsome. But Vido had something extra. The X factor, a tangible inner force that gave him an enviable vitality. Quite naturally, he projected an authority and a magnetism that Peter had never possessed. And right now, Vido seemed to be firing on all six cylinders, his whole body alive with energy and enthusiasm as he chatted to the lovely Camilla.

A twist of deep jealousy sealed Peter's fate. If she envied Camilla then she definitely didn't love Peter. Oh, sure he'd wined and dined her, and had flattered and charmed her—but on reflection it had been in a rather detached way which suggested he might not have been as interested in her as in her inheritance. Though she couldn't be sure. The one thing she did know, was that the engagement had to be ended tonight. It was only fair.

'I've seen someone I know,' she said, reluctant to claim a more meaningful relationship. 'Excuse me, I'll go over and say hello.'

Leaving the canapé plates in Joe's capable hands, she took a deep breath and went over to meet Peter. She could see his eyes darting about, taking in the luxurious room and its vibrant inhabitants. And then Vido's broad shoulders obscured her view as he moved towards her fiancé.

'You must be Peter Talbot,' Vido said coolly. 'Welcome.'

'Peter!'

Vido half turned to her, giving her a burning look over his shoulder before he managed to detach his hand, which Peter was enthusiastically pumping up and down.

'Hello, darling.' Peter gave her a perfunctory peck on the cheek as if she was an irritating diversion and turned back to Vido. 'I'm delighted to meet you at last, Mr Pascali,' he gushed. 'The City is alive with stories about your successes. I'm very interested in trouble-shooting myself. Think I'm pretty good at assessing my fellow man—'

'And woman,' Vido murmured.

Peter blinked. 'Oh. Yes. Of course. Mustn't forget the little woman!'

'Where would we be without them?' said Vido with a chuckle.

Anna bristled. Little woman indeed! This was a side of Peter she'd never seen. He sounded like something out of the ark! And was she imagining it, or was Vido deliberately egging Peter on?

'We'd probably be doing the typing and washing up, that's what!' Peter joked with a grin that was horribly close to being syco-phantic.

'I'd forgotten!' Vido said, slapping his fore-head. 'Remind me, Anna. It's my turn to do the dishes today. You were saying, Peter?'

Definitely, she thought darkly, he was stir-ring things and making Peter look stupid.

Though she had to admit that Peter was doing pretty well on his own, without any help from Vido.

'Er…yes.'

Peter had obviously been thrown by Vido's remark but he recovered quickly and Anna realised that her fiancé was revealing himself to be pretty thick-skinned. How odd that she'd never noticed before. Up to recently, he'd been charming and amenable, treating her with respect. Only after her grandfather's bankruptcy had he shown signs of regretting their engagement—and signs, too, of impatience with her.

Perhaps this was the real Peter. And she suspected that he wasn't bothered about her, now she had no fortune. Maybe he was an opportunist, currently latching on to the fact that through Anna he could land a plum job.

'Mr Pascali, I'm a great fan of yours,' he flattered. 'I wondered if we could have a little chat—'

'We must. But first there's someone on my staff I think you should talk to,' Vido said earnestly.

It seemed to Anna that Peter preened in delight at such personal attention. In vain did she try to resurrect her former opinion of her fiancé. Unfortunately the scales had fallen from her eyes and she was seeing Peter in a new light.

'Ah. Lucy.' Vido drew his cleaner into the crook of his arm and smiled down at her cheery face. 'Mr Talbot wants to tell you all about himself. Why don't you two get together with Joe and have…a little chat?'

Anna saw Peter goggling at Lucy's unusual outfit. She knew she ought to tell Peter that he was on the brink of selling himself to the cleaner and the gardener, but a wicked goblin seemed to have tied up her tongue.

It had annoyed her that Peter hadn't commented on the way she looked. He'd shown little interest in her at all. It looked as if she might be a stepping stone to his ambition— using her as Vido had, ten years ago. Cursing the ruthlessness and selfishness of men, she hardened her heart as Peter left with the amused Lucy.

'Why did you do that?' she asked Vido with assumed coldness.

'He was invited to support you, not to angle for a job,' he replied sharply. 'And he neglected to say how beautiful you were. So I'll say it for him.' He gave her a long and intense stare. 'You look fabulous, Anna.'

She stared, her heart pumping hard because his husky compliment had thrilled her. Then she recovered her composure.

'I must cook the pasta,' she said in a total panic and slipped out of the room before she melted into a little heap on the floor.

'Divine. What do you think, Vido, darling?' Camilla speared another piece of lamb.

Anna held her breath. It was crucial that he should like her cooking. Everyone else had raved about it—apart from Peter and Vido. Peter was too busy boring everyone with a résumé of his entire life and Vido, at the far end of the table from her, had been unusually silent as if something was on his mind.

The candlelight gave his face a soft, golden glow. He didn't even lift his eyes from his plate. 'Perfect.'

The conversation swirled around her again. While Condalita recounted a funny story to her, she watched him covertly. It pleased her that he was eating slowly, savouring every mouthful, especially the last. His eyes were half closed as if in bliss. Her pulses began to beat out a little rapid rhythm.

That's how he would be, she imagined, when kissing. Or making love. Suddenly he sensed that he was being watched and shot her a blazing look of such intensity that she felt it sizzle across the table like a flash of fire.

How dare he? she thought, angrily scowling at her plate. It didn't matter to him that Camilla might have seen. He didn't give a damn about anyone's feelings.

'Let's change seats!' cried Joe with a false heartiness.

Everyone, including Anna, fought back sympathetic smiles. He'd been sitting next to Peter and it was obvious why he wanted to move. But, amiably they switched around while some of the men collected dishes with Anna and she set off to the kitchen to turn out the chestnut cake.

When she returned, she found herself at the head of the table next to Vido. Trembling a little, she served the portions while Vido added crème fraîche or ice cream as requested. Squeals of delight greeted the first mouthfuls.

'Vido! This is the summit of a glorious meal. If you don't take Anna on, I'm leaving!' declared Camilla.

Thrilled, Anna found that her smile was tinged with bitterness. There couldn't be a clearer announcement of Vido and Camilla's relationship than that.

She saw Peter frown at the interruption. Tapping his fingers on the table, he waited impatiently till everyone had heaped praises on her head, reducing her to pink-faced embarrassment, then he launched forth again.

Eyes glazed over. One or two rolled up to the ceiling. She felt ashamed of his lack of awareness.

He'd spoiled the atmosphere. Without him, the conversation would have been light and amusing. For a moment as she'd looked around the table, which was sparkling with Georgian silver and crystal goblets, she'd felt wrapped in warmth and friendship, just as if she were part of an extended Italian family eating out of doors beneath clambering vines.

This was something she'd always craved during her lonely childhood and the cautious, reserved years that had followed. A dinner table bursting with interesting people who regarded her as their friend.

And one day, she'd dreamed of her own large family with her at its head, sitting beside an adoring husband. For a few magical minutes part of that dream had seemed a possibility. But it had been ruined by Peter.

Throughout the meal he had sought always to dominate. It was something she'd never noticed before. Even Vido listened to people. In fact, he spent most of his time listening with genuine interest.

She felt Vido's breath on her neck and she jerked her head around. 'Interesting. Your fiancé flashes his teeth a lot and flirts with Camilla, but he only addresses his remarks to the men around the table,' he mused.

Startled, she knew that he was right. 'Does he?' she dissembled, knowing perfectly well that Vido had spotted one of Peter's many flaws. Women weren't to be taken seriously.

She watched uncomfortably, wishing she'd never invited him. Peter was picking out as a target the unfortunate Joe, now on Anna's left, in the fond belief that Joe held some executive position.

'...*vis-à-vis* the international potential?' Peter queried pompously, waving a heavy silver fork in the air.

'No idea, mate,' the immaculately tailored Joe said cheerfully and Anna noticed with amusement that he'd suspiciously developed a Cockney accent. 'I'm only the bloke what mows the lawn.'

Everyone tried to suppress his or her giggles as the apparently innocent Joe transferred a morsel of food to his mouth with the utmost delicacy.

'The...*gardener?*' Peter said, aghast that he'd wasted his time on such a minion.

'Isn't this fun?' murmured Vido.

She ignored him, her anxious eyes on Peter. Clearly shocked and in need of a drink, he spotted Maria carrying a bottle of wine from the sideboard. Without even looking at her now, he held up his glass to her in a peremptory manner as if she were a servant. Vido tensed and there was an audible intake of breath around the table but Peter didn't even notice.

Anna realised that he saw Maria as an inferior. She was blonde and pretty and a woman in T-shirt and jeans.

'I can tell you about worms and dung heaps if you want to know,' Joe offered, all innocence. But Peter was too sure of himself to pick up on Joe's wicked insinuation. 'But *"vis-à-vis"* aren't my ball game. Ask Maria instead,' Joe suggested.

Peter laughed at what he imagined was a joke while Maria demurely poured wine into Peter's glass and batted her eyelashes at him, affecting a dumb-blonde expression.

'Maria,' Vido murmured into the hushed, waiting silence, 'is my head troubleshooter in Milan.'

As the white-faced Peter choked on his wine, Vido chuckled and leant towards the humiliated Anna.

'When we move into the drawing room for coffee and brandies,' he whispered into her burning ear, 'I think you'd better take your fiancé aside and have a little word with him about my philosophy regarding my staff. And then I want to see you alone.'

Grim-faced, she nodded. Peter could well have ruined her chances of working here. She felt like murdering him. Not only was she hopping with anger at his behaviour, but also she was appalled by her total inability to choose a decent boyfriend. Vido and Peter were both megalomaniacs. Why couldn't she fall for someone nice like Joe?

'I have a whole heap of things to say to Peter,' she said with a scowl. 'I'd like to go somewhere private with him if that's all right.'

Vido's triumphant expression unsettled her. 'Anywhere you like,' he murmured. 'Except the bedrooms.'

'No chance of that,' she snapped and he sat back in his chair looking horribly pleased with himself.

Their body language when they returned to the drawing room for after-dinner coffee told him all he wanted to know. Anna was flushed and on the edge of some kind of explosion, her eyes flinty with anger. Her breasts were rising and falling with her rapid breathing. She looked magnificent and utterly ravishable.

Peter, on the other hand, definitely had the relieved look of a man who'd escaped the scaffold. He was already contemplating Camilla thoughtfully and Vido put down his coffee-cup and smiled to himself as Peter accosted his PA and began to chat her up. She wasn't the sort to waste her time on vain men who had an inflated opinion of themselves.

The coast was clear. Fired with excitement of what was to come, he strode over to Anna and took her arm. She had removed her engagement ring, which she'd been wearing earlier. He felt a quickening of his pulses.

'I want to speak to you. My study. Now.'

Warily she looked up at him from under her lush black lashes. 'The kitchen,' she dissembled. 'I have to do the dishes—'

'No, I do. But we'll go there if you like. The kitchen will do just as well,' he purred.

Just then Peter broke off in the midst of talking to Camilla and held out his empty cup to Anna. Her eyes widened in amazement. Vido realised that Peter had learnt nothing from the earlier episode. It was clearly a deeply ingrained knee-jerk reaction. Empty cup or glass, woman near by, problem sorted.

'Coffee, Anna,' Peter ordered when Anna didn't move a muscle.

Vido's eyes narrowed. She fixed a totally false smile to her face.

'No thanks,' she said sweetly and swept out.

Vido's fists clenched. It would be very enjoyable, he thought, to punch Peter between

his nasty little eyes. Instead, he curbed his desire for violence and confronted the arrogant
brute instead.

'You may be my guest, but I would advise
you not to treat my staff, and particularly
women, like servants,' he said coldly. 'Get
your own coffee. Your legs aren't paralysed.'
He allowed a heartbeat of a pause before adding a menacing, *'Yet.'*

Steaming angry, he went to find Anna. She
was in the kitchen, scowling and nibbling
scraps of leftover lamb. Like him, she was
screwed up with anger and he wanted to kiss
her now, while she was in a raging passion.

Instead, he joined her and for want of a dis-
placement activity, he selected choice bits of
meat too. His temper receded slightly because
the flesh melted in his mouth and he was
standing almost hip to hip with Anna.

'That man is opinionated and insensitive and
he clearly regards women as a sub-species,' he
muttered.

'I *know*!'

Crossly she tore off a titbit but before she
could put it in her mouth he had taken her hand
in his and made her feed it to him. She gave
a little intake of breath at his temerity and he

almost crushed her to him, then and there, and kissed her till she couldn't breathe.

Unsteadily, he concentrated on what he needed to say first. 'My staff loathes him. He has as much chance of a job here as Vlad the Impaler.'

'He didn't seem like that before,' she defended, in case he thought she was terminally stupid. 'He was quite different—'

'Perhaps because you were an heiress,' he drawled.

She glared. 'Takes a gold-digger to know one,' she muttered.

His eyes flickered. 'Don't push it, Anna. I have the verdict on you,' he said, his voice softening. 'They like very much.'

She gasped. He gazed down at her small white teeth as they paused in savaging an unsuspecting piece of meat. Hazily he wished she was already nibbling at his flesh, instead. Soon, he promised himself.

'They do?'

He smiled at her amazement. Still the same lack of self-confidence. 'Their stomachs have spoken. They want you to be our chef. In fact, they're all deserting me if I don't employ you.

It's unanimous.' He gave a pretend sigh. 'Such is the lack of loyalty nowadays.'

Joy lit her face. 'Fantastic! Not the loyalty I mean... Oh. You were joking. Then...how do you feel about this?'

He managed a shrug. 'Your cooking is out of this world and you got on well with everybody, so we'll give you a short-term contract. OK?'

'Yes! Thank you!' she cried in awe. 'I can't tell you how thrilled I am!'

Show me, he thought, beginning to lose his head. But not yet, he cautioned himself. He cleared his throat. 'Here's a list of your duties and rough times of meals. I'll let you know what's happening each week so you can make plans. I'll notify you of any changes daily, during breakfast. You think you can handle your grandfather?'

Starry-eyed, she nodded vigorously. 'I'll break it to him gently. There's that beautiful convalescent home near by I told you about, that he's had a wistful eye on,' she confided. 'An old manor house, set in twenty acres with a lake. He'll love it. And when he's well enough to come here...' She lowered her eyes as if she wanted to hide her thoughts. 'I think I can persuade him to make the best of things.'

'I'm damned if I would in his place,' Vido observed.

'Your pride tends to take precedence over common sense,' she retorted.

He smiled faintly. 'You could be right. And I believe your common sense has surfaced at last. Concerning Peter,' he prompted, when she looked puzzled. 'You don't love him,' he drawled. 'Do you?'

'No.' She gave a little shudder. 'I'm sorry to have inflicted him on you all. He was an awful bore. And a prat. You brought out all his worst points.'

Vido lifted an eyebrow. 'He has some good ones?' he queried.

She wrinkled her nose. 'I thought he had. I liked the fact that he made no demands on me except...'

'Except?' Vido prompted.

'He liked me to cook for him and his business friends.'

'Hmm. And do you prefer an undemanding relationship?' he pursued.

Her mouth pruned in. 'I thought I did.'

His eyes flickered. 'But now?'

'I... Let's keep my private life out of this, shall we?' she said sharply.

'He can't come here again, Anna,' he warned.

'He won't.' And she burst out with the words he'd been waiting for. 'Our engagement has been broken off.' She frowned, clearly seething. 'To be accurate, he dumped me!'

'He what?'

'You heard,' she muttered.

'You're angry.'

Flashing silver eyes met his. 'Angry? I'm boiling! I was going to let him down gently but he got in first. He just said quite baldly that our engagement was over because he realised that I wouldn't help him reach his full potential!'

'And you said?'

'I was speechless! Then I told him I didn't know that had been my role because I'd been born in the twentieth century, not the nineteenth. And he said I had a lot to learn about men—'

Muttering something he didn't catch, she broke off. Stormed over to the sink and began to crash pans about. Her body quivered with appealing indignation.

'He's wrong. I've learnt enough for a life-time,' she growled.

But not about him, he thought. And he intended that she should discover every inch before dawn.

'I'm supposed to do those today,' he murmured, moving close behind her wonderfully supple back as it swayed this way and that in swift, economic movements.

'Well, I'm relieving you of that duty. I need an outlet for my temper—'

'Denting saucepans? I don't think so,' he said, putting his hands on her tiny waist and spinning her around. Now he would kiss her. Suggest they move somewhere more private. He smiled into her storm-washed eyes and said throatily, 'I have a *much* better way of releasing your passions.'

CHAPTER SIX

FOR a fraction of a second she resisted. Her body arched back, and he saw a look of shock on her face. Then he jerked her towards him and she came tumbling into his arms. His face bent to hers and he marvelled at how warm and firm she was. Hot and sweet, the blood in his body began to course faster through his veins.

His mouth closed over hers, stifling her muffled protest. Her lips opened beneath his. He groaned, his arms enclosing her more surely, one hand curved around a taut buttock and pushing her harder into his hungry loins, the other cradling the back of her head to drive their mouths harder together.

Suddenly he realised that she wasn't wearing any briefs. The thought made his insides turn over. There was a lack of inhibition about her that he'd never imagined.

Fascinated, he explored. Every move of his questing fingers rewarded him with an intimate knowledge of her curves. His hand splayed out to encompass her toned rear in its entirety and she moaned, jerking against him.

He devoured her. Kissed and nibbled. Let the tip of his tongue explore the line of her lips while her soft breath grew hotter with every passing second, teasing his flesh every time she gasped.

The silk of her hair slid seductively through his fingers like water. He kissed her eyelids. Across her brows. Down the perfect line of her nose. Lingered on the little channel above the lush bow of her mouth.

Gently his fingers drifted down the long line of her neck to the gentle swell of her breasts.

'No!' she whispered.

But contrarily she was melting against him, squirming and pushing her pelvis into his and inflaming him further. And then his fingers lightly brushed across one of her hard, inviting nipples and she let out a tell-tale moan.

'Anna!' he breathed, choking with desire.

Her fury and hunger exploded in one fatal moment. Helpless to stop herself, she lifted up her arms and drew his head down, kissing him with frenzied passion.

The touch of his fingers on her breasts was driving her wild. Gentle and insistent, the rhythm drummed into her body till it began to vibrate and open like a flower for him.

She didn't protest when he gently slid down her straps. With all the boldness of a true wanton she lifted both her breasts and offered them to him.

'*Dio!*' he breathed. 'You are so beautiful!'

She adored the way his voice cracked. Revelled in the look of bliss as he bent his head and gently took a throbbing nipple in his mouth. Her eyes closed from the sheer ecstasy of his sweet tugging and she pulled his hand from her hip and guided it to her other breast.

This was why people had sex, she thought hazily, as the incredible stabs of pleasure spread throughout her body. She suddenly wanted to feel his naked flesh against hers. With shaking fingers she tried to undo the buttons of his shirt.

He pulled away, his eyes dark with liquid desire. Moaning, she reached out but with deft movements he shed his shirt. Her fingers wonderingly touched his broad, golden chest and he quivered, tipping back his head as if her caress was unbearable.

Then he strode over to the huge pine table and pushed aside the discarded dishes with one sweep of his brawny forearm. Her heartbeat rocketed. Dry-mouthed, she tried to say something, to stop him before it was too late, but her conscience and common sense had taken time off and all she could think of was that she wanted him more than she'd ever wanted anything in the whole of her life.

He looked at her and she closed her eyes with a little moan of need. She heard him come close and she waited, almost screaming with the crucifying desire to be touched.

He took her face in his hands and kissed her fiercely with a roughness that she welcomed. Her mouth was coaxed open and she discovered what it was like to be kissed deeply, to feel the moistness of Vido's mouth and the unbelievably sexy caress of his tongue that was mimicking what she really wanted.

Her hands spread over the hard planes of his chest. Slid to his small buttocks, hard and taut beneath the gloriously tactile fabric. He muttered something into her mouth and then she was being scooped up and carried. The hard surface of the table hit her back. Her eyes widened.

The raw nature of his onslaught made electric thrills activate her nervous system. This was wild and wicked and she loved it.

Dark and impassioned, he loomed over her, kissing a path from her throat to each breast in turn and she bucked at the intolerable sweetness of his marauding mouth.

The weight of his body was wonderful. The movement of his hands tantalised her. Lightly at first, they caressed her calves. The soft skin behind her knees. She held her breath in anticipation and sank her teeth gently into his shoulder, working her way along it with slow thoroughness to alleviate her frantic physical ache.

The touch of his fingers had become even more delicate as they pushed up her skirt and glided up her thighs. She began to gasp. To cry out. To beg. But he didn't hurry.

She became angry in her frustration, savaging his throat with her mouth. And then she felt it. A light caress that made her freeze in delight. A furnace had been lit in her body, ignited by that one touch.

Slowly Vido's fingers slicked against the hard bud, bringing her to nothing more than a pleading, melting submission as she arched her body beneath his, doing everything she could to entice him further, to hurry him, to demand satisfaction.

His dark head lifted from her breast, his eyes as black as the darkest night.

'Anna!' he whispered as if caught up, like her, in unstoppable passion.

And then he slid down her body and she could feel the moistness of his mouth on the silk of her thighs before it enclosed her hot wetness and she completely lost all sense of time and place.

She bucked with involuntary movements. Heard dishes crashing to the floor. She growled her anger with him, wanting that hard male heat inside her, furious that he was depriving her of the one thing that she wanted. And yet...

Such exquisite caresses... Her head began to whirl. Sensation after sensation hurtled through her body. Every nerve was screaming, strung as tight as it could be. His hands were everywhere, reducing her to a mass of feeling, and all she could do was to tear at him and moan while delirium caught at her and finally pitched her to a peak of excitement, leaving her to gasp and pant as her body slowly climbed down and she lay beneath him, quivering and shuddering from each little ripple that rode through her like waves on the shore.

The world stopped spinning. He was kissing her. She felt too languid to do anything at all. It was a long time before she lazily opened her eyes and by then Vido's mouth had caressed every inch of her body.

She wondered if she'd been any good. Felt, surprisingly, no compunction at all at the hoydenish way she'd behaved. It had been what she'd wanted.

Except that now she wanted even more.

Tenderly his mouth touched hers. His hair was dishevelled, his expression touchingly bewildered. Supporting himself on muscular arms, he studied her for a long time and then he closed his eyes tightly.

'*Santo cielo!*' he breathed. 'What am I doing?'

She flinched, instantly hurt. He was going to tell her he'd made a mistake. In which case, so had she.

'You should know,' she glared, feeling horribly cheap.

'No, no, I didn't mean...'

Quickly he slid from the table and lifted her down with great tenderness. Her skirt fell into place and it only took a moment for him to slip her straps back over her shoulders. Though all of that was delayed because he kept dropping tiny kisses on her sulky mouth.

'I meant, Anna,' he explained, 'that I'd stupidly put you at risk. Anyone could have come through that door. It would have been very embarrassing for you. I apologise. I didn't think.'

Her heart started beating again. She smiled ruefully. 'You weren't the only one without a thought for propriety.'

'It...just happened. Before I knew it...'

'I know. Me too.' She took a deep breath. Tried to sound like a woman of the world as she concealed her soaring emotions. 'No big deal.'

He seemed taken aback. 'Er...no.' His hands were shaking when he reached down for his shirt and began doing up the buttons. 'It shouldn't have been here, though. That was clumsy—'

She stepped forwards and helped, astounded at her boldness. But he'd released something in her, a new confidence in herself, and she wasn't going to pretend otherwise. It had been great. And shocked though she was by her new-found assertiveness, she couldn't deny that she had hopes of it happening again.

'There was nothing remotely clumsy about what we did,' she said throatily. 'Apart from one thing.' She let him stew for a moment, her expression mischievous. 'I'm wondering. Will you,' she enquired, 'deduct the broken china from my wages?'

Vido laughed and held her close, his amused eyes gazing down at her upturned face. 'No. My fault,' he husked. 'I had no idea that we'd be so abandoned.' His fingers filtered through her hair. 'Regrets?'

Her gaze was steady. 'None.'

Except that he hadn't truly made love to her. Next time that would be rectified, she thought, and marvelled at her audacity. If she had a scrap of decency, she'd be appalled at herself. But she just felt elated—and oddly serene at the same time as if everything was going right for once.

'You were fantastic,' he breathed. 'I never dreamed...Anna, I don't know how long this will continue—'

'It doesn't matter.'

She met his eyes without shame. The only way to handle this was to pretend it meant nothing special. She needed to convince herself of that because way back there was a little nagging voice telling her that it had been a life-changing moment.

Whereas in truth it was just sex. A casual fling. Nothing more, nothing less. A guy like Vido didn't do commitment—and she wouldn't want that from him anyway.

'It'll burn itself out,' she said, sure of that fact. 'Until then—'

His eyes became sardonic. 'We light the touch-paper,' he said, brushing a thumb lightly over her breast, 'and self-ignite.'

Shuddering, she wound her arms around his neck and sank into a long and passionate kiss.

'We'd better wash up,' she whispered.

He nodded, his eyes brilliant. 'And then we can go to bed.'

Unsteadily, she pushed him away. The thought of falling asleep in his embrace was too sweet to contemplate, though it wasn't practical, of course. So she kept reminding herself that Vido was easing her physical hunger. And that was all.

In a quiet and companionable silence, they cleared up the broken china then stacked as much as they could into the capacious dishwasher and tackled the glass and silver together.

Hell, he thought. She'd been good. Beyond his expectations. Frowning, he admitted to himself that he couldn't resist her wholehearted abandon. Anna had been very innocent when he'd last known her. She'd clearly made up for lost time.

Heat permeated his pelvis. It would take a while before he got her out of his system—but it would be highly enjoyable while it lasted.

He was just wiping down the surfaces when a loud yell came from the garden outside, so loud that they even heard it over the noise of the throbbing dishwasher.

Anna exchanged startled glances with him then they both hurried to the garden door. She stopped in surprise.

Peter was rolling on the ground outside in a tight ball, swearing like a trooper. And watching him, a champagne glass in her hand and a cynical expression in her eyes, was Camilla.

Vido's girlfriend.

Anna gasped, her hand going to her mouth as it dawned on her what she'd just done. She could feel the blood draining from her face and wanted to stamp with rage at her stupidity. She'd been so overwhelmed by Vido's horribly skilful seduction that she'd totally forgotten that he and Camilla were in some kind of a relationship.

But *he* couldn't have forgotten, she thought furiously. He'd used her like a sex toy to amuse himself—without a thought for Camilla's feelings.

Ready to explode with rage, she couldn't even look at Camilla. Guilt and shame and fury swept over her in sickening succession. Almost weeping with the horror of it all, she let her hair swing forward as she bent down to Peter and put a hand on his shoulder.

'What is it?' she asked in a harsh croak.

She was rewarded with a glare and a string of oaths. Shocked, she straightened and flung a wary glance at Camilla, who was now smiling at Vido wryly. Anna noticed that he wasn't in the least bit bothered by the embarrassing situation.

'Looks an interesting scenario. Are you all right, Camilla?' he asked in amusement and Anna felt her contempt for him soar sky-high.

He's just made love to me! she wanted to yell. He's a cheat and a liar and doesn't deserve either of us! She trembled, appalled at how easy it had been for him. One sultry look from him and she'd virtually torn his clothes off. Humiliation burned inside her, turning her stomach to acid.

'...couldn't be better, darling,' Camilla was saying airily. 'I've been wanting to do that all evening.'

'Do what, exactly?' Vido asked with a laugh.

Camilla hesitated. 'Thump Peter.'

Anna's eyes widened. 'You...hit him?'

'We-ell...To be accurate, his genitals came into contact with my knee. He'll be all right though, in an hour or two,' she conceded.

Vido grinned. 'How did the...er...accident happen exactly?' he said with a chuckle.

Camilla looked over to Anna doubtfully and Anna heaved in a long rasp of air. This was turning out to be a terrible evening.

'He made a pass?' she suggested flatly.

'Afraid so.' Camilla rubbed her breast rue-fully.

It was too much. Both of the men Anna had become deeply involved with had been hell-bent on treating her like a moneybox. Grim-faced, she gave Peter a push with her toe.

'You arrogant, thick-skinned rat!' she cried, half-hysterical with fury and the sickening misery that coiled and untwisted in her stomach. 'You only went out with me because you thought I was to inherit a fortune! And when my grandfather lost everything, you faded out of the picture—till I rang you about the interview and you thought I might be useful after all—'

'Anna—'

'Leave me alone!' she yelled at Vido, flinging off his restraining hand.

This was history repeating itself. What was the matter with her, that men should treat her with such contempt?

'Be glad you've found out what he's like,' Vido said soothingly.

'Oh, I'm glad!' she spat, whirling on him. 'Glad that I know where I stand. I was only a means to an end. No one important. Not when there are other fish to fry. Other women to enjoy.'

Vido frowned, clearly sensing that she wasn't just talking about Peter. He opened his mouth to comment but she spun away, too upset to speak, too choked with emotion to look at his lying, cheating face. He'd turned her into a cheap one-night stand while the woman he adored had been only yards away. No wonder he'd been appalled when he'd realised Camilla might have walked in on them.

This was what happened when you gave in to desire, she thought miserably. Heaven help her. How was she going to survive six months in the company of a lecherous, cheating bastard like Vido?

'It's been a tough day for you,' remarked Vido with infuriating sympathy.

'You can say that again! I've discovered how low a man can sink!' Spitting tacks, she glared at him and then at Peter, who was struggling to his feet.

'I'm ashamed to say that I have an overwhelming urge to kick a man while he's down,' Vido observed. 'I suppose, however, I'll have to help him to his car. Won't be long.'

Without ceremony, he grabbed Peter's arm and led him off, protesting.

'I'm terribly sorry.' Stiff and pale with dismay, Anna felt she had to apologise to Camilla.

'Not your fault!' Camilla stared curiously at Anna's quivering lip. 'Hey! No harm done to anything important! Just Peter's pride and his dangly bits.'

Anna blinked back the tears of shame, her mouth quirking up for a brief moment until she remembered how she'd betrayed Camilla and the huge burden of guilt descended again.

'Oh, this is awful!' she groaned.

'Poor Anna. You must feel doubly betrayed by the men in your life,' Camilla said gently.

Her eyes widened as her stomach plummeted. Had she guessed that Vido had made love to her in the kitchen just now?

'What do you m-mean?' she stuttered.

'I know what happened between you and Vido.'

'*What?*'

Anna's knees gave way. Scarlet with shame, she sank to a low wall, shaking uncontrollably. And the awful thing was that Camilla came to sit next to her, hugging her as if she didn't mind that Vido had made love to another woman at all.

'I understand that you believe Vido was fortune-hunting, like Peter, when you were teenagers,' Camilla said, brushing back Anna's hair behind her ear.

'What was that?' Confused, Anna tried to see what that had to do with Vido's infidelity to Camilla.

'He told me. What happened between you two. When you were at school.'

'Oh! That!' Anna croaked.

'I know you two misunderstood one another. You've got *him* wrong. He'd never do anything like that. He's far too moral. You'll realise that when you've been here a while. He's straight and honest and a man of absolute integrity. I know. I've worked with him for years and know him through and through. He's a wonderful guy, Anna, and would never treat a woman badly. He has too much respect for them.'

'Camilla—'

'No. Listen. Frankly, I think the two of you have got the wrong end of the stick about each other. Keep an open mind. You'll see I'm right.'

Anna thought how passionately Camilla spoke about Vido. But she hadn't heard all the tales about him or heard him admit that he'd told his friends he was desperate to make money—and didn't care how he did it.

'I understand why you think the world of him.' Anna looked into the woman's friendly eyes and felt a heel. 'The evidence says otherwise.'

'Tittle-tattle from schoolgirls?'

'My grandfather, too.'

'Ye-es. Well, we'll agree to differ. Peter, however, did use you,' Camilla observed gently. 'I can see how the realisation of your fiancé's betrayal must have brought back memories of the time when you and Vido fell out. The difference is that Peter's a louse and you're well rid of him.' She smiled. 'You're with people who care about you now. Don't let Peter ruin your life. He's not worth it.' She smiled. 'I know a man who is.'

Anna bit her lip. Camilla idolised Vido. She was blind to his faults. But she couldn't blame her. Once she'd thought he was God's gift too.

'You're one of the nicest people I've ever met,' she said, silently pleading for forgiveness. Her slumped body straightened. 'You're right. I won't let this spoil things for me.'

'See you at breakfast, then?'

She managed a weak smile. The guilt curled inside her stomach, making her feel sick. 'Sure. But...if you don't mind, I'll slip home now.'

'I'll walk you back.' Vido had appeared just behind her and she tensed at the sound of his voice.

'No! I want to be alone!' she muttered, leaping up in frantic confusion.

'You're not walking along that lane at this time of night on your own,' he insisted. 'Not in that state.'

She glared at him from under lowered brows. He'd helped to put her in 'that state'!

'Goodnight, Camilla,' she said shakily. And was surprised and embarrassed to find herself being hugged. Over Camilla's shoulder, Anna's eyes met Vido's in a hard, misery-filled stare.

'Piece of advice just in case you bump into someone you know,' Camilla murmured. 'Take the piece of rosemary from your cleavage. And Vido, smooth your hair and put the correct buttons in the buttonholes of your shirt.' Giggling, she turned and disappeared into the kitchen.

Anna had frozen, her face ashen. 'She knows!'

He was sheepishly sorting out his shirt. 'Apparently.'

Anna felt the nausea rise to her throat. The man was devoid of all moral feeling. Her instincts about him had been right. And Camilla must love him so much that she had decided to turn a blind eye whenever Vido strayed! Disgusted, she turned on her heel and started marching through the garden to the side gate.

Behind her she could hear Vido hurrying to catch up. She began to run and as she did so the tears began to prick hot and spiky behind her eyes. Please, she muttered to her faltering self-control, don't let me cry!

'Something's wrong. What is it, Anna?' he demanded, catching her wrist and swinging her around.

Wrong? No, she'd just been ravished by another woman's lover! Nothing unusual. Apparently not where he was concerned, anyway. Appalled, she bent her head. Let her face be obscured.

'I'm tired,' she snapped. 'I want to go home and I want to be left alone.'

Cruelly, he swept back her hair and tipped up her chin. Knowing that her eyes were moist with tears, she met his gaze defiantly. And almost sobbed aloud at the look of concern on his face.

'I knew it. You're very upset. This has gone deep, hasn't it?'

She hated the mesmeric, soothing quality of his voice. If she didn't know better, she'd think he really cared. Whereas he was probably hoping to keep her on a string, handy for those odd moments whenever he felt randy.

'As a well,' she choked accusingly. 'So leave me alone.'

'But I want to comfort you—'

'I bet!' she muttered.

'Anna, you're angry with me. I don't understand. What is it that I have done? We...' He hesitated, then continued. 'It was fantastic, making love to you. We both agreed that we'd enjoy one another without any strings attached and—'

'Vido,' she grated, barely able to hold back her temper, 'I'm exhausted. Goodnight.'

Puzzled, he walked behind her till she reached the cottage. Waited till she had let herself in. Then he trudged back, trying to understand why she'd taken out her anger on him.

If she hadn't been so hostile he might have taken her to bed. He would have made love to her and helped her to forget the pain of being rejected by that prancing idiot, Peter. He would have shown her that she was beautiful and desirable. As it was...

He heaved a heavy sigh. Perhaps there were other reasons for her sudden coldness towards him. He had to think this through.

Quietly he bade his goodnights to those of his staff still chatting in the drawing room before they departed for the weekend, then he went up to his suite for a long, icy shower. Followed by a sleepless night trying to understand the complex workings of Anna's mind.

CHAPTER SEVEN

THROUGH the dark hours till dawn, Anna's thoughts had run non-stop. She'd even stumbled out of bed, wide awake and weary, and watched a late-night film on television, only to discover that it was highly erotic and contained scenes that made her blush.

Unable to bear seeing someone getting the satisfaction she'd been denied—even though the woman was just acting—she switched off the television and stamped up to bed again with a mug of hot chocolate.

For the next few hours she considered giving up her job. Then argued her way back into it. Everything about it was perfect—apart from the unfaithful Vido—and why should he and his lack of morals ruin things for her?

It also gave her a sense of grim justice that she should use him as he'd intended to use her. So she'd take his money, enjoy the work and being with his staff, and then walk out of his life, as free as a bird.

As for emotions, they wouldn't get a look-in.

The decision made, she did manage to snatch a few hours of sleep. At six-thirty she let herself into the house using the code that Vido had given her to override the security alarm.

She spent a calming time picking soft fruit for breakfast and arranged it in a beautiful bowl she'd found and was just making apple bread when Vido appeared, wet-haired, bleary and barefoot, and wearing a white towelling robe that contrasted wonderfully with the honeyed glow of his skin.

Her heart thudded. Ruthlessly she pulled in some deep breaths to control that unsettling mix of lust and anger that he aroused so effortlessly.

'Anna!'

He looked genuinely surprised to see her but rather wary. When he headed straight for her, she threw him a cool glance.

'Morning.'

He came to a halt. The word would have iced a lake. With a sense of shock, Vido knew then that his conclusions in the grey, small hours had been correct.

Peter's betrayal, so soon after their love-making, had reminded her that she could never trust anyone. Not even the man who had so thoroughly explored every inch of her and had unselfishly devoted himself to her pleasure.

His body contracted. A haze came over his eyes as he recalled the sweet hunger of her sensational body. He thought of his high emotion, the unbelievable feelings he'd experienced for the first time in his life. His fierce need to possess her utterly. The unbearable ache when she'd turned him away from her door.

And his ensuing anger. He frowned and stalked over to make himself a coffee. Whilst making love last night, he reflected, her mistrust of men's motives had been suspended for a short time. Perhaps this was purely because she had desired him. And so he had found his way through her cool reserve and her closed emotions, to the passionate wanton who lay beneath. His senses stirred with the memory as he fumbled with the coffee grinder.

It had surprised him when she'd suggested they should have sex for as long as they wanted. It had been 'no big deal'. She had 'no regrets'. Whereas now…

What was she playing at? Last night had been so good. He pushed his hands through his wet hair in confusion, furious with her for being so contrary.

Her casual attitude to his lovemaking had been a totally unexpected reaction. What was he—a stud? To be brought out of a drawer when passion flared and then tucked away till needed again?

'You're very quiet,' he ventured sharply.

'I'm busy.'

The venom, the contempt, turned those words into missiles. His eyes hardened. She hated anyone touching her emotions. And when they did, she retreated into her cold little world and let her spiteful streak emerge.

Annoyed, he stirred his cappuccino. He didn't like women who played games. Nor did he like being bracketed in the same class of insensitive, selfish oafs as Peter.

He watched her covertly as she slid a cake tin into the oven. And he veered wildly between grabbing her there and then and subduing her to his will—or leaving her strictly alone till she came begging.

Anna was uncomfortably conscious of the thickening of the atmosphere as Vido scrutinised her every move. It seemed her body sprang into life whenever he was near and it was a constant struggle to conquer her physical response to him. Common sense told her that he wasn't worth all the effort that her hormones seemed to be exerting.

Searching for a tablecloth, she felt daggers of hostility being hurled in her direction. Somehow she willed herself to stay calm as she carried the cloth to the pine table, the scene of her humiliation.

And, she thought with grudging honesty, the scene of her initiation into the joy of sex. She flushed, her lips parting as her breath came high in her throat.

'The table looks different this morning,' he drawled.

Her mouth tightened at his deliberate reminder. 'It would. It's daylight, for a start,' she said and floated the gingham cloth onto the table, shutting out the wonderful images that pestered her mind. Vido, his body poised over hers. His eyes dark and molten. Then nothing but glorious sensation.

She gulped and collected the French stick for the One-Eyed Jacks. And when she sliced it, her knife strokes were venomous.

Vido decided that he would not let her put him in the wrong for what had happened. She had wanted him. He would remind her of that later. When she begged for him again. His heartbeat accelerated till he could hardly breathe.

Anna was determined to stay inside her shell. And he was equally determined to get her out of it again.

'After breakfast,' she heard him say, as he settled himself comfortably on a kitchen chair, his toned, golden-brown thighs far too visible for her comfort, 'I want to discuss the kitchen design with you.'

There was nothing she'd like less. 'Better still, I could come up with a design and you could decide what you want to keep and what you want to change,' she suggested, her calm reply giving no hint of her dislike. 'You'd be able to get some work done after breakfast then.'

'There's nothing that won't keep,' he persisted. 'We must do this together.'

She shrugged as if it meant nothing to her either way and slapped two pounds of pork and apple sausages on the worktop.

'If you insist.'

'I do.' Vido wandered over. She could smell his skin, freshly soaped from the shower. 'How many people are you catering for?' he asked casually.

'Twelve.' Her eyes widened. She'd just realised that they'd been thirteen for dinner the previous night. No wonder it had been a disaster!

'Anna—' He put his hand on hers and she shot him a keep-off glance. Which he ignored. 'There's only us. It's Saturday.'

She looked at him blankly. 'Us? You mean...?' A blush touched her cheekbones at her own stupidity. 'My day off? I don't need to be here!' she muttered. Picking up the sausages, she stomped over to the fridge.

'I was surprised to see you,' he admitted. 'But now you're here, it makes sense to choose the kitchen units together. The fitters are coming soon and we must have everything organised or it'll be months before they can slip us into their schedule.'

She heaved a sigh of irritation. But she could do this. It might be good for Vido to discover that his charm would get him nowhere where she was concerned.

'Fine,' she said with crisp decision. 'But I'm seeing my grandfather after lunch.'

'I think we'll be finished by then. You will be paid for the overtime.'

His tone had been silky. She threw him a suspicious glance but he was sipping his coffee, his lashes dark on his cheeks.

'Good.' They'd remain businesslike. If he came near her, she'd warn him off with a volley of well-chosen words. 'I've done some soft fruit for breakfast to start with—'

'Would you like tea or coffee?' he asked with worrying pleasantness.

'Tea,' she grumped.

With her back very erect, she collected the cutlery and china and arranged the settings so that they were each at one end of the long table.

Vido's mouth curved into a smile when he eventually returned with the pot of tea for her. 'Very baronial. Or are you afraid I'll leap on you before you've finished your first cup and test the table in daylight?'

'Don't be ridiculous!' she scoffed. If he tried, she'd hurl china at him.

'In that case...' He brought everything to the place beside her. 'It's easier like this. We can talk without the need of a telephone,' he explained.

She tried a withering look on him and dipped her spoon in the bowl of fruit. Lush strawberries, sweet raspberries, plump loganberries and huge tayberries. Gorgeous. Tasting the exquisite sweetness of the fruit, she beamed with pleasure.

Vido shifted in his chair, sending a faint waft of lemony soap in her direction. 'Last night,' he began in a throaty voice.

'It was a mistake. I don't want to talk about it.'

His jaw dropped and she took some pleasure in his surprise. 'A...mistake?'

She froze him with an arctic glare. 'You know it was.'

'I know it was mind-blowing. I've never known anything like it. I felt as if you'd taken me halfway to heaven—'

'Now we're back on earth again,' she grated, fighting her desire to say 'did I?'.

Of course he'd say that kind of thing to every woman. That was what men did. Vido had flattered her all those years before—and every word had been a downright lie.

'I thought we were going to indulge ourselves.' He wouldn't let this go. 'Have a casual fling.'

His eyes narrowed. It dawned on him that she'd virtually fallen into his arms only minutes after Peter had rejected her. He went cold. He'd caught her on the rebound. What an idiot he was.

'You thought wrong,' she said stiffly. 'It was a mistake. I was overwrought and—'

'Yet afterwards I remember you were perfectly cool about continuing our purely sexual relationship,' he said, barely hanging on to his temper.

His mind was racing. It seemed she might have used him for sexual gratification, to prove that someone desired her. In the name of heaven, she was a calculating little madam.

For a moment he had thought... Fool. Leopards didn't change their spots.

The look she gave him hit him straight between the eyes like a blow from her fist. 'That was before we came across Camilla and Peter. I realised I shouldn't have let you near me. It's too much to expect you to feel remorse, I suppose.'

The anger in her virtually blasted its furnace heat at him. 'Remorse? What the hell for?'

'If you don't know,' she said in a cutting tone, 'I'm not going to tell you.'

'And if you keep suppressing those erotic passions of yours,' he drawled, finding himself aroused by her wildfire, 'you're going to explode again in spectacular style.'

'When I do,' she retorted tartly, 'it won't be with you.'

'I wouldn't take bets on that,' he slurred.

She shivered at the threat there. He was furious that she was turning him down and that wretched pride of his was urging him to prove her wrong.

'I'll make the Jacks,' she muttered, desperate to get away from him.

She stamped holes in the bread and put the pan on to heat. The back of her neck prickled as the hairs rose. Vido had come to stand close behind her and she found herself breaking the yolk of the first egg she cracked, in her agitation.

'Let me.' The husky whisper rippled through her nerves in waves. His arms came around her, the pressure of his body hard and warm.

'Don't do that!' she grated, squirming from the release of agonising need. She loathed herself for having these feelings for him.

'Just cracking the eggs for you,' he said evenly and slid each one into the centre of each piece of golden bread. Then he walked away, leaving her horribly ragged at the edges.

It was all she could do to make a show of eating. The relief when he went off to dress was like a cold shower of rain. Grimly she cleared the kitchen, listening all the time for his footfall.

When it came, she was writing menus for the week ahead. She tried not to notice how snugly his jeans fitted. Or how the black T-shirt hugged his body. Instead, she put aside her papers and coolly began to study the design books he'd brought as if he had no effect on her whatsoever.

As they discussed, agreed and discarded various options, she noticed that his fingers were gently moving backwards and forwards across the silky surface of the table. The sensuality of the movements began to seep into her almost as if he were stroking her skin. She could almost feel the pressure and as her body responded she had to bite her lip to stop herself from groaning.

The memory of his touch haunted her. The intimacy between them now embarrassed her profoundly. She couldn't help remembering where he had touched her—and to what effect.

But she said nothing and continued with her chilly replies to his suggestions until it was time for her to go home for lunch.

He estimated how long she might stay at the hospital visiting her grandfather. After showering and shaving, and changing into a fresh cream shirt that matched his clean jeans, he drove down to her cottage, feeling angrier than ever.

The whole day had been wasted. He'd done nothing—except churn over and over in his mind everything that had happened between them.

Whatever he did, he saw the flow of her features and the lyrical language of her hands and body. Hating to be so possessed by her, seething from the challenge she presented, he vowed to break open that hard shell of hers once and for all in the only way he could. With sex.

Outside the plank door, he drew a deep breath and gave the bellpull a yank.

She'd been sunbathing. Her face was flushed and glowing, her glorious body fighting to remain decent despite the small white bikini.

'How's your grandfather?' he enquired politely.

Glowering at him, she half hid herself behind the door. 'Fractious. They're doing tests. But his speech is still not good. He keeps trying to tell me something that's troubling his mind and...' Her voice cracked. 'He—he cries when he can't get the words out.'

'It must be hard for you, seeing him so helpless,' he said.

'Terrible,' she admitted.

And he was in the house before she could say any more. 'Brought the design books for you to check,' he announced, putting them down on a rickety table. Though he didn't mention that he had his toothbrush in his back pocket as well.

She looked startled and frightened, her eyes as dark as charcoal. Yet he noticed with a catch in his breath that her nipples had become hard and erect. He groaned. She wanted him as much as he wanted her. And this time he wasn't going to take no for an answer.

'Thank you.'

Muted and sullen, she hunted around for a way of escape but he stood in the middle of the room and he knew she was too proud to run from him.

'I thought you'd like to mull over what we decided,' he said quietly, trying not to keep his gaze from straying below her neck. But he knew his desire must be evident on his face because she swallowed and licked her lips. 'I want to be sure,' he added huskily, 'that you're happy with everything.'

'Right.'

With that breathy whisper, she absently shut the front door.

He smiled at her lazily, projecting the promise of what was to come. Her hand went to her mouth and he saw the swelling of her breasts and the lengthening of each peak.

Needing to keep cool, he wandered into the kitchen, murmuring, 'I wonder if it's changed since I was here. Oh, yes. It's considerably tidier—and cleaner!' he called back.

Anna couldn't stand there any longer with virtually nothing on. She knew that he'd noticed what was happening to her body and despaired that it had betrayed her. He'd imagine she would lie down for him, she thought angrily. And hated him more than ever for making her so defenceless against his charms. And against her own alarming lust.

It was like being hooked on drugs. And possibly as dangerous.

'Let yourself out!' she cried loudly, and ran upstairs to find something—anything—to cover herself.

At the sound of his footsteps on the spiral oak stairway that led straight into her bedroom, she froze.

'What…what are you doing?' she squeaked.

His dark head appeared, dipping beneath the low beam. The broad shoulders. Chest, hips, legs. And now he had taken a step across the oak-boarded floor and was looking at her with unnerving intent.

'What do you think?'

Reading his intentions, she backed away but in her panic she forgot the uneven floorboards, which dipped and swelled like miniature hills and valleys from centuries of gently shifting joists. Before she knew it, she'd fallen back on the counterpane of the big four-poster bed and

Vido was hovering over her, his eyes black and gleaming.

'This,' he murmured, his hands pinioning her arms to her sides, 'is an invitation I can't resist.'

'It's not an invitation!' she blazed, wriggling frantically. 'I fell! Get your hands off me! I loathe you! Despise you—!'

'Want me.' His kiss interrupted her tirade, softening her briefly until she dragged her brain back into her head and struggled beneath him. To her dismay, that only dislodged her bikini top, exposing her hungering breasts to the gaze of his lethal black eyes.

'I don't want you!' she whispered in futile denial. Her mouth was opening to his and she was half sobbing in her desperate attempt to remain indifferent.

'Your body does.' He took a nipple between his lips and sucked. She moaned and bucked beneath him.

'But not my brain!' Her eyes seared his with hatred.

'It's just sex,' he reminded her cynically.

'So lie back and enjoy it!' she scoffed.

'Why not?' he urged.

'Because you're a two-timing rat like Peter and whatever you're used to, personally I don't like sharing!' she jerked, wriggling like an eel.

They rolled on the bed, every contact with him a torment, every swoop of his voracious mouth causing delight and fury.

'When,' he growled, between repeated tugs at her horrifyingly eager breasts, 'have I two-timed?'

Gasping, she pushed his head away and shuddered as his hands slid to her hips. 'All your life!' she spat. 'As a teenager, and now. What if I rang Camilla and told her what you were trying to do right at this moment?'

He frowned. Lifted her back to the pillows and held her there, his expression uncomprehending.

'Let's take this in order. I never went out with more than one girl at a time when I was at school—'

'They said different!'

'Oh, Anna!' he sighed irritably. 'That was gossip. Idle chatter from man-hungry girls with too many hormones raging about. You only have their word.'

But every female sighed over him. They all wanted him. Would he really have turned them down?

'Loads of girls said you'd made love to them—'

'There were two—and those were some time before I dated you.' He frowned. 'The others made extravagant claims about me so they could be seen as part of my set. I had no desire for a string of sexual conquests. Or, rather, I had the desire but I didn't want a cheap and unsatisfying relationship. Besides, I had no time to date at all, after my mother was sacked,' he added grimly.

'You stayed out all night. That's a fact.'

'Yes. I went to your grandfather's factory straight from school—'

'I know,' she said coldly, remembering how he'd tried to cheat his fellow workers out of their holiday savings. 'The shift ended at eleven.'

'And I,' he said tightly, 'worked the next shift through the night till early morning painting cheap and ugly models of Shakespeare's birthplace. If you don't believe me, I'll show you my pay chits. And you can marvel at the pittance I was paid,' he added with some bitterness. 'Hell, Anna, how do you think I could spend the nights with a woman when I was bent over a workbench painting nasty souvenirs? Do you think I'd have the energy even to rush off to someone for a five-minute quickie? I was too exhausted to do anything other than drag myself to school in the mornings and fall asleep during lessons. I had to make money. I didn't care how—and I was prepared to slave in that dump in order to do so.'

He saw the truth filter into her mind. The lowering of her lovely eyes as she realised that she'd misjudged him.

'Was that what you meant?' she asked shakily. 'About doing *anything* to make money?'

'Well, I certainly wasn't planning on a loveless marriage,' he said coldly.

She let that go, knowing for a fact he was lying. 'Didn't anyone at school know you were working in Grandpa's factory?' she demanded. 'Is that why they were convinced you were with a woman every night?'

He scowled. 'I wasn't exactly proud of what I was doing.' The hardness of his eyes made her shrink into the depths of the bed. 'Anna, my mother brought me up to respect women.

The ones who deserved respect, that is,' he added, flicking her a sardonic glance.

'And the ones who didn't?' she pursued.

'I steered clear.' His eyes flickered. 'I had no wish to contract some sexual disease,' he said scathingly and she flinched at his cutting reminder of the accusation she'd flung at him. 'Why would I lie about this?' he asked grimly. 'What would be the point?'

She seemed to waver. And then her head snapped up again in challenge.

'It doesn't alter the fact that you've treated Camilla abominably!' she cried.

'You've lost me.'

'Don't pretend to be dense! Camilla! Remember her?' she cried, sounding almost tearful.

'What about her?' he asked irritably.

Her jaw dropped. 'You are a b—!'

'Don't say it!' he hissed, his eyes glittering with anger. 'I may be illegitimate but I don't like it being flung in my face every time you're feeling vindictive.'

'You're in a world of your own, the way you turn things so they're someone else's fault!' she stormed. 'Let me *go*. I'll call her and tell her just what you're trying to do to me!'

'Go ahead,' he gritted. He reached out for the phone on the bedside table and handed it to her. 'I can guarantee she might even be pleased.'

Anna gasped. 'What are you saying?'

He shrugged. 'She knows there's something that draws us together despite our dislike for one another. Camilla is a very perceptive woman and she cares about me—'

'The poor deluded woman! She's so dazzled that she'd *share* you?' Anna flung, her eyes hot embers in her pale face.

Vido frowned. 'Share? What the—?' The penny dropped and he grinned, his eyes kindling as he realised what she was implying.

'Don't you smile at me!' she stormed.

Laughing a little bitterly at her low opinion of him, he kissed her hard, fighting with her mouth when she tried to bite him. Such passion. It would all be for him. He groaned at the thought.

'Anna,' he said thickly, 'Camilla has never found her way into my bed, let alone my heart. Since she arrived here she's fallen head over heels for Joe.'

Anna frowned, pushing away Vido's tormenting fingers as they caressed her breasts. No. That wasn't right.

'You're lying,' she scorned. 'I distinctly heard you tell Camilla you adored her.'

'I do!' He gazed at her innocently as if that was perfectly normal behaviour. 'It doesn't mean we're lovers.'

'She calls you ''darling''.'

'And everyone else,' he pointed out. 'It's a manner of speaking. But she loves Joe. Ring her. Ask.'

She had to know. And if he was lying, she thought grimly, she'd ram the phone down his throat.

'Number.'

He dialled it for her, his hard-boned face uncomfortably close to hers, his breath whisking hotly over her mouth. When she heard Camilla answer, she suddenly felt stupid.

'Oh. Hello. It's Anna,' she stumbled.

'Darling! How are you?' Camilla called gaily. 'Enjoying your freedom from old prune-face?'

Anna hastily controlled a wry smile at the irreverent reference to Peter. 'I—I wanted to get something straight,' she said, glaring at

Vido as he remorselessly kissed along her jaw-line.

With one hand she tried to push him away but he clasped her fingers in his and kissed her erect nipple instead. He scared her. There was anger in every line of his body.

'Fire away,' she heard Camilla say, somewhere in the hazy distance.

'It's about Joe,' Anna jerked out, the blood coursing through her veins.

'Darling Joe.' Camilla sounded soft and dreamy. 'Isn't he divine?'

'You—you and he... I mean...?'

'Clever you! I'm in love with him, Anna. Madly. I want his babies. Is it that obvious?'

'No, no.' Anna gulped. She'd made a dreadful mistake. It seemed that all her reasons for mistrusting Vido were vanishing—except the fact that he'd stolen money from the factory workers. That was in no doubt. Her grandfather had certain proof. But...it seemed he wasn't promiscuous or two-timing after all. Her stomach swooped. 'Can I get this clear? You and Vido aren't...' Her voice tailed away in embarrassment.

'I see what you're getting at!' Camilla laughed. 'Darling, he's all yours. I adore him of course and he adores me—naturally because I'm so adorable—but we're not right for one another. Whereas Joe, lovely, hunky, gorgeous Joe...'

Vido took the phone from Anna's limp hand. 'Bye, Camilla,' he said abruptly and put it down. 'Satisfied?' he muttered. 'Because if not, you soon will be.'

She bit her lip and flushed, her eyes wide with dismay. 'I'm sorry!'

'More.'

She squirmed. 'What else can I say? Everything pointed to you two being more than fond of one another. I *heard*.'

'And jumped to conclusions. Again. You thought that I was the kind of guy who'd make advances to you while sleeping with another woman.'

He let his anger show. She had to know that he objected violently to her mistaken assessment of his character.

'Yes,' she whispered.

His mouth tightened. 'Thanks. But one at a time, is my motto. Today, it's you. Tomorrow, who knows?' he sliced. 'But you can be sure I'll let you know when *we're* finished.'

She winced. An odd pain filtered across her eyes. Of course. She couldn't stand rejection.

'I can only say that I'm very, very sorry,' she husked.

'And you will be punished.'

He thanked his lucky stars that she was sexually experienced. It made it easier. He was going to enjoy this. No strings. Just physical release at last.

'How?' she croaked.

Her breasts were full and thrusting forward, dark nipples aroused and urgent. He was bursting with desire but he wanted this to be different. Long and slow and deep. He let his mouth move over her breasts, his lips savouring the change from the smooth satin skin to the puckered flesh surrounding each hard, rosy centre.

'You,' he breathed, his voice thick with wanting, 'are going to spend the entire evening and night pleasuring me till you can barely move for exhaustion.'

CHAPTER EIGHT

HER entire body seemed to catch alight. Fierce fingers of delight stabbed at her and she let out a moan before she knew what she was doing.

Vido brought his mouth down on hers in a fierce kiss, the pressure of his kiss deepening the throb of her pulses deep inside, the caress of his hands gently hypnotic.

Every part of her screamed for satisfaction. And this time she meant to get it. Sinking beneath the passionate onslaught of his mouth, she felt herself drifting towards that delicious intoxication which had allowed her to surrender her inhibitions and enjoy the movement of flesh against flesh, lip over skin, teeth grazing bone.

Yes. She would have it all. Her fingers slid down to the button of his jeans. Firmly he pulled her hand away.

'No.'

Thwarted, she frowned at him. 'I want—'

'It's not what you want, Anna. It's what I want.' He rolled onto his back and pulled her on top of him. 'Make love to me,' he ordered softly.

Her eyes narrowed as anger flashed through her. But he was spiralling a finger around her breast, his mocking eyes challenging her, and suddenly she knew what she would do.

In a quick, lithe movement, she slid away. Pulling open a drawer in the tallboy, she located two silk scarves. He wanted to be pleasured. She'd do her best—with the help of the film she'd watched. And she'd end up pleasuring herself.

'Hand,' she ordered in a croak, helplessly aroused by what she intended.

He swallowed, hardly believing what he'd heard. Impatiently she flicked one of the silk scarves like a whip and he realised that she was serious. Eyes dark, his chest rising and falling with quick, sharp little breaths, he held out his hand. Every nerve in his body tingled. He could hardly bear the suspense.

She was tantalising. Her face had become very solemn in concentration as she tied his wrist to the post of the bed. Her small pink tongue had slipped between her lips in a sweet, endearing way that made him want to hold her tight and nestle his head against hers.

And yet he could sense the passion and tightly controlled appetite behind her serious exterior. Voluptuous in every movement as she strolled to the other side of the bed, she seemed almost as excited as he was.

Her breasts rode high above her sucked-in stomach—drawn in, he believed, from tension, not vanity, because her lips were parted and little spurts of harsh breath whispered through them.

'Hand.'

That was barely audible. Just a pained rasp. His throat dried. He closed his eyes at the exquisite ache that had claimed him. The silk slithered over his wrist and up his arm.

No... He opened his eyes. It was her hair, slipping and sliding till his skin seemed alive with sensation.

'Anna! Kiss me!' he breathed.

Through the swollen rosiness of her lips, she whispered, 'Wait.'

She paused, staring at him, the smoky haze of her eyes melting every bone in his body. Then biting her lip, she straddled him and he could feel the heat of her burning into his abdomen as she slowly undid each button of his shirt.

Pushing it open with shaking hands, she let her fingers wander over his jerking chest muscles while he fought to stop himself from groaning out loud. Her breasts filled his vision yet he couldn't touch them. Straining up with his mouth, he attempted to catch one dark-tipped nipple with his tongue.

Imperceptibly she leaned lower and allowed herself to be teased by the tip of his tongue; first one breast and then the other. She tasted salty and he realised her skin glistened with moisture.

Eagerly he lapped, desperate to provoke her so that he could take charge again. Because he wanted her. Now.

Her head went back and she moaned, the glorious length of her neck achingly vulnerable to him. Then she wriggled down his body and pushed off his shoes and socks in frantic haste.

Stretching as far as he could, he reached out his left foot and made contact with her satiny stomach. She shivered and let out a little mew of pleasure, moving closer so that he could explore.

He felt the slight weight of her breasts, delighting in their soft, sensuous roundness. His toes brushed across the hard peaks and she writhed wantonly.

Desperate to hold her, he tugged at the silk that confined him but the knots only tightened.

'Release me,' he growled in a voice not his own.

'No. You—wanted—this,' she jerked.

He looked down and saw the dark cap of her head and the gleaming smoothness of her beautiful shoulders. Then with a few deft movements she had stripped off his jeans and briefs.

He closed his eyes again, willing himself not to ejaculate. She didn't touch him. A groan of need escaped him. The silence, the waiting, was driving him crazy. What was she doing? Every pulse in his body thundered painfully. He was rigid with imposed control, his muscles quivering with tension.

And then it began. A slow, wickedly delicious tremor that ran over the surface of his skin. The caress of her hair against his straining hardness. The lightest fingertip touch over his pelvis. The moist enclosure of her mouth around his nipple.

'Anna!' He fought his way to reality and forced his heavy lids to open. 'I can't hold on. Set me free—'

He shuddered. Stared into her drowsy eyes, his heartbeat leaping uncontrollably. The pleasure was intense. Her hand had slid down his hips and was inexorably moving to his hard arousal.

And then she shifted her weight, slipping off her bikini briefs impatiently as if she couldn't bear to wait any longer either. He watched her settle just above him and he pushed his hips up in desperation so that he could feel her soft, wet warmth.

With a shudder, she impaled herself on him, deeper, deeper, as he struggled to hold back, frantically counting the stars on the canopy over the four-poster till even they began to blur and combine.

Because she was kissing him and the sweetness of her mouth touched every heartstring in his body.

'Oh, Anna! Anna!' he whispered, greedily devouring her mouth as the pressure in his loins became more intense.

'You want me!'

It was a statement, not a question. He answered by thrusting hard at her and she gave a delighted shudder, the rapture on her face totally destroying his self-control.

As he quickened his movements, she did so too. And suddenly he felt the squeeze and quick release of her internal muscles, hard and sharp, over and over again until he was mentally climbing the wall with pleasure.

He thrashed about the bed, groaning, feeding on her mouth, nibbling angrily at her because she controlled the pace and he wanted to climax before his muscles gave out in exhaustion from the savage tension he was putting them under.

But he hung on. Because her delight stunned him. He was pleasing her again and that gave him a kick and a strange sensation of satisfaction that he couldn't begin to understand.

She could hardly breathe. The storm inside her body was driving her on, some inner knowledge telling her when to pause, when to continue, when to tighten her pelvic muscles to produce that look of delirium on Vido's face that had turned her heart to jelly.

He was pleading. Whispering lyrical words in his own language. She took his face in her hands and kissed him deeply, overwhelmed by her own feelings. And then sat back, her eyes fixed on his as she sought the final satisfaction.

Speared on him, every inch of her a mass of sensitised nerves, she suddenly wanted his full co-operation. Lunging forward, she tore at the knots, muttering desperately when they failed to release. And then he was free.

With a gasp, he flipped her over and his beautiful weight sank on her eager body. She gave herself up to the wonderful sensations inside her. Her eyes closed, her lips parted and she began to pant and beg for more, more, more.

Hot and hard, he thrust inside the sweet, hungry core, jerking and bucking like her. Dimly she was aware that they were almost fighting their way over the bed, her foot or hand or naked buttock occasionally feeling the hardness of one of the posts.

It seemed she didn't know which way up she was, let alone where, as the tension built to an unbelievable height and she felt she was boneless, bodiless, all her senses concentrated in one place.

No. Two. Her heart yearned for him too. Longed for love. To be free to adore her lover.

Bitterness touched her briefly because she knew that was impossible. The man she loved would never have Vido's flaws.

And then he lifted her up, pushing her legs around his strong back, and she was lost to the world of sensual sensation as he plunged deeper and faster and she felt the incredible spasms rocket through her body one after the other in hard, rolling, unstoppable waves.

For a moment she seemed to hang in mid-air, then she became aware of her breathing and his, the gentle, sweet taste of his mouth on hers, the shuddering of his body as he carefully lowered himself to distribute his weight and then she knew the slow quietening of her body.

She smiled. Her smile was kissed from corner to corner. His head nestled into her neck and his lips were soft and warm there.

'Anna!' he whispered brokenly.

Trembling at the emotions that pelted through her head like rain, she stroked his head. It had been good sex, she kept telling herself. Nothing more. Plenty of people did this and didn't confuse gratification with love. It was just her stupid, romantic brain that wanted it to be more than raw pleasure.

Yet the longer she lay there in his arms, listening to his rapid heartbeat gradually slowing, hearing him breathe, rejoicing in being held, the stronger her yearning for love grew.

'I think,' she said croakily, needing to break away from her dreams, 'I'll have a shower.'

'I'm environmentally friendly,' he said, taking her face in his hands and gazing at her intently. 'Let's save water together.'

He saw the flash of pleasure that lit her eyes and that parted her lips in a small gasp. It ripped through him, too. He was bewildered. He'd never felt like this before. Not this...raw tenderness. He fought it. Not wanting it.

Their shaking fingers linked. Before he knew what he was doing he had kissed her long and sweet, the kiss of an adoring lover. He shut his mind to what he was feeling. Great sex. He had what he'd wanted; her total capitulation. All that remained was the matter of clearing his name of the theft.

Hell. He'd forgotten to make her confess while she was in the throes of passion! He swore under his breath. Next time. A wry smile tilted up the corners of his mouth. The problem was that everything went from his head when she was in his arms. Poor mis-guided fool that he was.

Wrapped in his embrace, her body had become limp and pliable. Hardly capable of breathing, he picked her up and carried her to the bathroom.

In the tiny room, she stood before him, naked and painfully beautiful, her huge eyes wide amid their fluttering fringe, her skin so flawless that he could only stare at her in reluctant awe.

'You're unbelievable,' he husked.

Tears filled her eyes.

'Anna!' He looked at her helplessly, not knowing what he'd done.

'I'm OK.' Her fists knuckled away the threatening tears and she turned, walking to the shower, her tight rear capturing Vido's fascinated eyes. Looking back at him over her shoulder, she said with a shaky laugh, 'It's just that I've finally accepted I look all right, after all those years of being a hag.'

He felt the pain tighten his mouth and curl hotly in his stomach. It was no wonder that she'd hated the world she'd lived in, and had become contemptuous of people. Perhaps anyone in her position would be bitter and resentful and full of spite.

As he stood there, with the sound of the shower dimly penetrating his mind, he tried to kick back the emotion that had shot like a fountain to fill every cell in his body. No emotion, he told himself. No pity. Enjoy her.

Joining her, he gently soaped her body as he might that of a child. She was strangely meek and listless, in contrast to the abandoned woman who had aroused him to such intense heights only moments before.

Obediently she lifted her arms when directed, turned and stood still while he took a heart-stoppingly tender pleasure in what he was doing.

'Out you go,' he said huskily, his throat thick with emotion for this child-woman, this siren-innocent. 'Dry yourself. I'll be with you in a moment.'

Quickly he lathered up and showered off the suds. She seemed to be in a dream, her hands vaguely dabbing with the towel, so he took over and dried her before pushing her back into the bedroom to dress.

And then it dawned on him. *Dio!* he whispered, stopping short.

They'd taken no precautions. It had happened so quickly. He had something ready, in his pocket, but she'd taken over and he hadn't given it another thought...

Dannazione! There was a danger that she might become pregnant!

He froze with shock. Not because he was horrified, but because he'd felt a wild leap of joy that she might be carrying his child. Hell. He really did want to be a father. Badly enough to accept even someone like her as the mother of his baby.

To his bewilderment he found himself smiling. Saw in his mind's eye, Anna cradling a small infant, her soft eyes full of joy as she looked up at him and said, *Vido! Look, our baby!*

He groaned. Rigorously he punished himself with a fierce rasp of the towel over his aching body. Wished he'd never begun to think about babies because there was a terrible yearning inside him that he knew wouldn't be quieted.

He was building castles in the air and making Anna his princess, because he wanted to be a father so badly.

Except... His spirits sank as his logic took over, reminding him that she was sexually experienced. That had been made very clear. So it was likely she and Peter had been lovers when things were going well between them— and she could still be on a contraceptive pill. Which was why she'd had no qualms about making love with him, and why she hadn't asked if he had any protection.

He swallowed, a terrible misery filling his throat. That meant there would be no child. He felt stunned. The possibility had made him so happy for a moment...

Giving himself a stern talking-to for being a sentimental fool, he strode firmly into the bedroom and dressed, ignoring her where she sat brushing her hair. He needed to get his head sorted about this.

Anna loathed him but she liked sex. That was the only reason they were together.

Therefore, they would have fun. She would learn—if not to like him—at least to respect him. And then he would extract her apology and they'd part in due course. Anything else, any attempt at finding a heart inside that gorgeous body of hers, he realised, might be a disaster.

He couldn't allow himself to believe that his tender longing for fatherhood had anything to do with Anna. And no way was he going to embark on a proper relationship just because he was broody.

'I'm hungry,' she said, oddly shy when he looked up at her. 'Shall I cook something?'

He nodded, his face serious and thoughtful. 'Sure. Why not? I'm ravenous.'

'Seafood risotto? I have enough for two.'

'Great.'

He felt slightly ridiculous. They were talking like polite strangers. But when she began to cook, he felt the old warmth creep through him. Together they dunked the shellfish in a basin of cold water to disgorge the sand then scrubbed the shells with a stiff brush. Quick and adept, she knocked off the barnacles from the mussels and tugged off the beards then set him to wash everything in several changes of water.

Happily she hummed as she sautéed some onion and herbs. Every move she made was fluid and graceful, the total economy of a skilled chef.

While the stock was simmering, he poured out the wine and handed her a glass.

'To pleasure,' he said quietly.

Her eyes were veiled. 'Pleasure.'

Determined to make the most of her, he kissed her moist lips. And went back for more. 'You blew me away, again,' he said thickly, his finger running down her delicate cheekbone.

She blushed, a reaction he hadn't expected. 'It was this film,' she mumbled.

He blinked, perplexed. 'Film?'

'Uhuh. I watched it last night. I—I couldn't sleep. There was this man and this woman and...well, it involved scarves,' she finished lamely.

He frowned. After a long and heavy silence he tilted up her chin. She wouldn't meet his eyes. A suspicion formed in his mind.

'Are you saying you've never done anything like that before?' he asked, his throat taut.

Her lashes fluttered. 'I've never...been with a man, let alone tied him up! You're my first lover,' she confessed in a whisper, the blushes sweeping up her face in rosy waves. 'You must have realised!'

He couldn't believe it. But he knew it was true. And her confession had changed everything.

'Why did you do it?' he jerked out harshly.

Silver-grey, her eyes flicked up to his and then away again. The blushes were multiplying.

'Because I wanted you,' she husked.

'I mean, why the scarves?' he croaked, completely confused.

'I wanted to be...' She bit her lip and let her hair fall forward in that old, heart-tugging gesture that always got to him, every time. 'To be good. Memorable. Because you'd made love to so many women...' And she broke away to fiddle with the pans on the stove.

Vido stood stock-still, her revelation hammering in his head. She'd been a virgin after all. No contraceptive pills, then. God help him. She could be pregnant with his child after all.

In which case, they would have to marry. No kid of his would be brought up a bastard. But it would be born of lust and little more.

Silently he cursed Anna then. For bewitching him. For being so innocent that she'd had no idea how far she'd pushed him till it was too late.

Anger gripped him. He ached to love and to be loved. To create the miracle of a child with a woman he adored. Yet it looked as if he might be heading for one of the worst situations he could imagine: a marriage without love.

And yet…he studied her subdued figure as she sliced scallops and added them to the rice. Hell. His brain was all over the place. She seemed terribly vulnerable, her face set in anxious lines, her fingers trembling.

A profound emotion coursed through him. Tenderness, affection, yearning. His heart went out to her. Despite everything, he had to comfort her. He went over and drew her into his embrace.

'Oh, Vido!' she whispered helplessly into his neck. 'You must think I'm an awful Jezebel. I won't do it again—'

Helpless to resist, his mouth crushed down on hers. 'Oh, yes, you will!' he muttered and felt a wild delight when her eyes lit up and she smiled at him as if he'd made her deliriously happy.

What was happening to him? His feelings were bewildering in the way they chopped and changed. As he stroked her glossy hair, he tried to get his thoughts clarified.

Despite everything, he cared about her. Anna was more innocent than he'd imagined.

She hadn't known what she was doing when she'd teased him like a practised wanton.

And perhaps misery, and the honest belief that he'd betrayed her in the most despicable way, had driven her spite in the past. Gossip at school and her own poor self-regard had made her believe that he couldn't possibly have been interested in her.

The consequence was that she had accepted what others had claimed—that he was after her money. After being brutalised for so many years by people making fun of her, that must have been a terrible blow to her esteem. Hence her act of spite.

Maybe she wasn't perfect, but who was? Holding her like this, he felt more passion for her than he could handle. She made his emotions hurtle around as if they belonged to an adolescent boy.

It dawned on him that if she was pregnant then perhaps he could *learn* to love her. To make some kind of life for their kid—should there be one. He should at least try. His vendetta must end.

He kissed her again. His heart was thumping hard. By committing himself to Anna he could end up getting hurt. But he had no choice. He couldn't take the risk that—if she did give birth to their child—she and that evil old man Willoughby would bring up the kiddie. He might not get a look in on his own flesh and blood. That was unthinkable.

He'd work at the relationship. And if there was no child... His teeth clenched. Then he and Anna would be free to leave one another whenever they wished.

CHAPTER NINE

VIDO seemed almost tender towards her that evening and she adored every moment. They fed one another like proper lovers, sipped one another's wine, and kissed often.

Curled up with him on her sofa and watching a late-night film—in case, he said with a twinkle in his eyes, there was an interesting technique they might learn—she felt her heart softening as every golden hour went by.

And later they went to bed and made slow and gentle love, which was sweeter and more tantalising than anything she'd ever known.

Only one thing nagged at her. This time he'd used a contraceptive. It had been something she hadn't thought of before. She felt a little sick at the thought that she might have conceived. She'd been stupid. It wouldn't happen again.

But...a baby...And instead of feeling horrified, she found her heart lurching with crazy delight at the wonderful thought of carrying Vido's child.

She smiled wryly. It was too late to turn back the clock. It was doubtful that she'd conceive so easily. Some people took years to do so. She put it from her mind, vowing that she would take what happiness she could. Enjoy life for once.

The next morning they walked to Stratford along the path they'd often traced when they were at school together. The years seemed to fly away. As they walked they talked, and it all came back to her; how easily they'd fallen into an immediate rapport, how comfortable she'd felt with him when she'd been ugly and undesirable and he'd been the most handsome guy in school.

It reminded her of her role in his life then and now. As a young girl she'd only had her inheritance. This time she had nothing to offer but her body.

Sadly she reflected that this was all he wanted. Not her, not her mind and inner self. Just her physical shell, where once it had been her money. He was flawed, and as shallow as ever, and she'd better remember that.

This relationship was going nowhere. Better that she kept her feelings under wraps and stayed aloof than she abandoned herself to him and ended up sobbing her heart out one day.

'Great weekend,' he said casually.

That was all it was to him. A bit of fun.

She looked towards Holy Trinity, where Shakespeare was buried. The church was romantically positioned on the river bank amidst the weeping willows. Shakespeare knew a thing or two about treachery, she thought. And love and life. If only she were more worldly, she might cope better with her contradictory feelings.

'Great,' she agreed calmly.

He put his arm around her and kissed her hard, then and there. She found herself melting into him. Body, mind, heart, soul. Desperately she tried to stop herself from thinking she was in a dream.

Because you always woke from them.

'Hello, you two. Have a good weekend break?' Camilla burst into the kitchen on the Monday morning, followed by a cheerful-looking Joe.

Anna went pink as she lifted cinnamon bread from the oven but fortunately Vido spoke for her.

'Excellent. Paid our respects to Shakespeare and his family in the church. Had lunch in The Dirty Duck surrounded by actors being actorish, and the afternoon we'll draw a veil over. You?'

Camilla grinned. 'Similar.' She hugged Anna. 'So pleased. Look after him. He's worth his weight in gold.'

Anna gave a faltering smile. She wished that could be true. Because she had loved every minute in Vido's company. Because they could be companionably silent, or laugh themselves silly. He could be deeply romantic and tender, or hot and passionate and demanding.

And yet his heart wasn't engaged at all. Whereas she knew that, despite all her efforts, she had fallen irrevocably in love with him.

Emotion clogged her throat. She had to get a grip on herself. Vido was just a bit of fun. Time she cooled things down and tucked her heart away where it couldn't get hurt.

Gradually the breakfast table filled up. Everyone talked at once, describing their weekend activities. Vido amiably wandered back and forth, providing coffee for his staff as if he were a tea boy.

'Smells wonderful. When's it ready?'

She felt her knees go weak to find Vido so close beside her but she managed to put a chill in her voice. 'Just about now.' Pointedly she moved away.

'You OK?' Following, he gazed down at her, his eyes narrowed in sharp assessment.

'Of course. I'm concentrating,' she answered coolly and pushed past without looking at him.

Aware, however, of Vido's frowning gaze on her, she dished up the Spanish omelettes, receiving a hug from Joe on the way.

'Marry me!' Joe declared expansively. 'Or, at least, chain yourself to my kitchen table and cook for me forever!'

Vido's head snapped up. 'You can make do with what you get during work hours!'

'Sense of humour failure, darling,' Camilla said with a laugh.

He swept a chilling glance over her. 'Time we got down to business,' he muttered. 'We have eight key workers from Lucas and Duke coming here tomorrow. For those who don't know, they're one of the top advertising agencies in the country. I think I've identified where their problems lie but I'd be glad of your input as usual.'

'How many do I cater for?' Anna asked, matching his cool tone.

He turned his hard gaze to her. 'Twenty for lunch and dinner for the next three days,' he informed her abruptly. 'You'll have two agency cooks to help you and we'll all chip in with the fetching and carrying. It'll be interesting to see if any of their key workers help. I want everyone to listen, observe and to get involved.'

'What about you moving to the flat here, Anna?' queried Steve. 'Need any strong arms?'

'Good idea. I suggest you and Joe supply her with boxes and whatever she needs,' Vido directed. 'Anna, you'll be free after lunch to pack. Steve and Joe will move your stuff in the van. But we'd better discuss menus when you've finished your breakfast. I'll be available after coffee for anyone who wants to talk over my report on Lucas and Duke.' He rose, his meal virtually untouched.

'Lost your appetite?' frowned Camilla, eyeing him warily.

He gave her a cold stare. 'Trying to curb it,' he replied and strode out.

For a moment there was a tense silence and then the others all started talking at once. Anna managed to answer remarks addressed to her but she couldn't eat either. Eventually they all drifted away and she began to stack the dishwasher.

'Menus.'

Her stomach flipped as he strode in like a whirlwind and dragged out a chair by the table. But she gritted her teeth and turned to the furious-looking Vido.

'Menus.' She brought her cookery books to the table and placed her notebook in front of her before sitting down opposite him.

'What the hell are you playing at, Anna?' he asked grimly.

'Menus,' she muttered.

His thumb and forefinger turned her chin so that she was forced to look at him.

'We were perfectly civilised yesterday. And yet today you're as icy as the North Pole,' he growled. 'You're worse than a weathervane.'

'We're at work.'

'It's more than that,' he pursued. 'Isn't it?'

She managed to push his hand away. 'If you must know, I don't want you to get the wrong idea.'

'About?' he asked, his eyes as dark as a thundercloud.

'I like the sex,' she said frankly. 'Very much. But I think it was a mistake to spend the weekend together.'

'You didn't enjoy it?'

'I didn't say that. Just that we ought to re-member this isn't a normal relationship.'

'How very modern of you,' he drawled. 'I hadn't realised you wanted wham, bam, thank you ma'am.'

He wanted to shake her. But instead he'd go all out to change her mind. His eyes gleamed. It would be a battle between them. Anna and her cold heart, versus him and his determina-tion to make her want him in every way imag-inable.

'Is that agreed?' she asked.

He reached out a finger and traced it down the side of her face. She quivered. He left his seat and kissed her neck. With a groan, she wound her arms around him and pulled his face around so that she could kiss him.

'Sex. Nothing else,' he murmured, looking into her startled eyes.

'Uhuh.' She could barely speak.

'Better get on with those menus,' he drawled, unsure if he'd won a victory or not. But he'd work on her. Every hour of the day.

He regained his seat and she started turning pages haphazardly. Then she looked up. 'I've decided to keep my cottage and rent it out,' she said. 'I'll need it when the six months are up.'

His mouth tightened. So she was planning on leaving then. It felt as if she'd stabbed him in the heart. 'Wise move.'

She felt disappointed. What had she expected? That he'd get down on one knee and declare that he didn't want her to leave then because he loved her? Which she wouldn't have accepted—or believed—anyway. It baffled her why she was so stupid where Vido was concerned. Hadn't she been hurt enough?

They planned the meals in a series of frosty monosyllables and then he left her, his retreating back taut with tension, saying it all. Although Steve and Joe kept her in stitches with their banter while she was packing, she missed Vido dreadfully.

During dinner that evening she kept catching his eye. Every time she did, curls of pleasure rippled through her. It dawned on her that she was hooked on him and longed to be an important part of his life. Instead of which, she was a temporary sex-toy. And she hated herself for being incapable of walking away from her own degradation.

She'd wandered into the garden after dinner, taking her coffee with her. It was an attempt to get away from Vido's suffocating personality. She needed space and freedom to remind herself of his failings so that her love for him could be crushed.

Male arms came around her. Teeth nibbled her ear. 'Come,' Vido growled harshly. 'I have something to show you.'

And like a fool she went, holding his hand, following him up the twisting servants' stairs and along the corridor that led to the east wing that had been derelict when she'd lived there.

The carpet was thick and springy beneath her feet. Hand-painted silk lined the walls, occasional tables held graceful vases filled with scented orange blossom and sweet peas from the garden.

'I need you.'

He looked at her and she felt her bones softening. How she loved him. If only they could be happy together, live here, bring up a family...

She bit her lip and tried to shut her stupid dreams from her mind.

'This,' he said, accompanying his words with a hard, possessive kiss, 'is my suite.'

The heavy panelled double doors swung open. She stared in awe. The sitting room stretched away, high-ceilinged, light and airy and with a stunning view over the lush gardens towards the lake.

Closely monitoring her stunned expression, he drew her after him and then, after hesitating for a moment, he swept her off her feet before she could protest and pushed his way through a second set of double doors.

To his bedroom.

'No, I—'

'Yes.'

Grim-faced, he stopped her mouth with his. Roughly deposited her on the huge four-poster bed. Drew the heavy brocade curtains so they were enclosed in a small world of their own.

And proceeded to make such exquisite love to her that in the darkness afterwards, when he'd fallen asleep, she cried silently, shaken by his tenderness.

For hours she stared into the blackness, his arms still around her, his breathing regular as if he had no worries on his mind at all.

Reaching out, she drew back the curtain a little. A shaft of moonlight illuminated Vido's face. In repose his expression was one of contentment. And his dream was obviously enjoyable because he was smiling.

Desperately loving him, she touched his tumbled hair and moved closer to breathe in his breath. If only he wasn't so tender in his loving. If he had taken her without any sweetness at all then she might have coped. As it was, she loved him more and more. And all her determination to stay aloof was flung to the winds the minute he had touched her lips with his.

It would be hell when he tired of her. Perhaps, she thought blushing at her own boldness, she'd better make sure he never did.

'They seem happy.'

With his champagne flute, Vido indicated Ben Lucas and Tom Duke, splashing in the subtly floodlit pool on their last night at Stanford House.

'I'll say. Thanks to you, their business is on course again,' Anna pointed out from her lounger. And she covertly admired the gleam of Vido's toned body in the silvery, soft moonlight.

She stretched and sighed, smiling to see everyone having such a good time. It was like the end of term, she thought—though she'd never been involved in any of the impromptu parties at school and had watched wistfully from the sidelines.

'Tired?' Dark-eyed and watchful, Vido reached out and touched her solemn mouth with his forefinger.

She trembled. 'Not as tired as you must be. You've wrought a miracle these past few days.'

Granted she had worked hard that week catering for the people from the advertising agency—but Vido had worked harder, poring over videos and notes of his meetings with the employees and management and socialising with them all. In the early hours he'd come to bed exhausted but he'd wanted to make love to her and she had been as inventive as she could.

She blushed to think of the things they'd done.

'They just needed to remember to sing from the same song sheet,' he said, his lazy gaze hot and hungry as it wandered slowly over her body.

'It was more than that and you know it,' she replied thoughtfully.

'Tell me,' he murmured.

'Vanity?'

'No. I want your honest assessment.'

'Well...' She'd been stunned by some of the things he'd said in the course of his summing up of the problems besetting the agency. 'Where do I begin? There's so much. You were amazing. You got them all to see what they were doing; bitching and competing and playing stupid mind games. They saw how you operated. That you listened to your staff with genuine interest and acknowledged their contributions before making your own comments. They came here stressed out and miserable— and now look at them!'

They both watched everyone cavorting like kids on a spree. Anna felt quite unsettled by her admiration for him. He'd been straight, direct and compassionate. She thought of the awkward situations he'd defused with humour and tact. Laughter had played a big part in getting everyone to lighten up and admit to their own foibles. No wonder Camilla and the others worshipped Vido.

'More!' he drawled.

She didn't mind stroking his ego. Every ounce of his considerable energy had gone into the saving of the agency. No wonder he looked shattered—and oddly vulnerable.

'Let me see. I thought your observations were tough but always fair—and you framed them in such a way that no one could take offence. I think you opened their eyes to what they'd been doing. That manipulative woman, for instance, who cried every time she was— quite rightly—reprimanded for shoddy work.'

'I'm convinced she didn't even realise what she was doing,' he mused. 'I think she'd probably been resorting to tears all her life. You could see how quickly it made her boss back off.' His eyes were very intent on her. 'Go on.'

'I liked the fact that you laid great store on treating staff with respect and seeing their point of view. And that without giving a lecture or seeming harsh, you showed everyone better ways of working. *Your* ways.

Democracy rules.' She slanted him an amused glance because he was smiling to himself as if her words had some special meaning. 'What is this sudden need for adulation and praise?'

'Once you thought I was the scum of the earth,' he reminded her quietly. 'Suddenly I'm Mary Poppins.'

So that was it. There had been a purpose to all this. He was making her admit she'd been wrong about him.

'I was young and sensitive to hurt. You'd treated me badly.'

'You thought I had,' he corrected. 'So I'm not evil through and through any more?'

Perhaps not evil. But not the kind of guy she could entirely trust. That made her sad. How could she love him truly without trust?

'I was only pointing out that you're good at your job,' she said stiffly.

'Thanks,' he drawled but he looked disappointed that she hadn't answered his question and she was glad when a couple of the agency staff came over to chat to him.

Lying back in the steamer chair, she watched his easy manner, the obvious awe in which everyone held him. Grudgingly she had to admit that he was more than good at his job; he was exceptional. The gratitude of the staff of Lucas and Duke had been touchingly emotional, from the two once-warring directors to the timid tea girl who had been the butt of everyone's malice.

There was a quickening of her pulses. *Could* she have misjudged him? Restless, she stood up and went over to refill her champagne glass. As she was doing so, Vido appeared at her side.

'We'll have more time to ourselves for a couple of days,' he said quietly. 'I'm looking forward to that. We need time together.'

'In bed,' she muttered, a little resentfully because that was all he wanted.

'That. And out of it. I like being with you, Anna. I like talking to you, just walking with you and being in your company. I like shopping with you and organising the week. Everything.'

Her eyes shone. It was more than she'd ever hoped for. But she wondered if she was being foolish and decided that she'd been hurt too often to let her soaring emotions surface.

'That's nice.' Casually she lifted her glass to him, trying to conceal her trembling. 'To your expertise. In so many fields.'

He crooked up an eyebrow. 'Hmm. Haven't tried a field yet.'

Despite herself, she giggled. 'Doesn't the grass in front of the summer house count?'

'No,' he said firmly. 'Must be a field.'

'Without cows and cow pats.'

'Tonight, then.'

She smiled and began to think of the things she could do with a blade of grass.

Three weeks later they were enjoying a post-theatre party in Stanford House. It followed a successful session where Vido's talent and sensitivity had turned another bickering clutch of directors with clashing egos into a dynamic and enthusiastic team.

There had been an almost family atmosphere when the directors and Vido's staff had all met up at the Royal Shakespeare Theatre for a production of *The Taming of the Shrew*. And the performances were so funny that their helpless laughter had created an even firmer bond between them all.

In the dark of the theatre, Anna had held Vido's hand and, between laughing, had felt incredibly happy for him that his business was such a great success.

And now she was really wavering about Vido's character. Watching him chatting to the eager directors, who had become willing recruits to his fan club, she had begun to seriously doubt that he could ever have acted without honour. Perhaps the school gossips had been wrong. Her grandfather too.

Except...she couldn't believe he'd been interested in her as a person, not when she'd been so ugly.

'Verdict?' murmured Camilla, curving an arm around Anna's waist and nodding at the animated Vido.

'I don't know,' she said honestly.

'For a sensible, feet-on-the-ground person, you're incredibly dense,' Camilla said with a sigh and drifted off to answer an insistent telephone in the study, the long skirt of her elegant gown trailing behind her.

Anna hitched up the skirt of her own rose-coloured dress and moved closer to Vido. She pretended to sort out the buffet but in reality she was listening to his conversation—just because she loved to hear his voice. There's love-sick for you! she told herself wryly. And felt a tingle of joy when he detached himself from the group and came over to her.

'Not tired with all this standing?' he asked, his eyes solemn.

A little surprised, she laughed. 'I'm not an invalid, Vido.'

'No,' he said quickly, lowering his gaze. 'Of course not—'

'Vido!' They looked up, alerted by Camilla's expression.

'Trouble?' Vido asked.

'I'll say. Just had a call from Barncoat's,' she said. 'You're not going to like this. Their shares are in free fall and they want you, pronto, Superman.'

Vido muttered a curse under his breath. 'I was looking forward to a break. Can't Batman go?'

'Washing his Batmobile.'

'OK. Come and help me pack, Anna,' he said with resignation.

Her face fell. 'Pack? Are they some distance away, then?'

'New York,' he threw back at her as they headed into the house.

Dismay brought her to a halt. New York! He'd be gone for ages. As she bunched up her silk skirts and ran to catch him up, she tried to stifle the urge to cry. That was silly. He'd be back.

Gloomily she trudged into his suite of rooms, only to be caught and lifted into the air. 'What—?'

'I need you,' he muttered. 'I'm going to miss you more than I can say.'

He was already sliding his hand up to her thigh and she was groaning, every fibre trembling as his skilled fingers aroused her.

And afterwards, when he'd thrown things into his case and rushed out with a curtly uttered 'bye', she lay on the bed and stared blankly at the Tudor carvings that decorated the sturdy posts.

Was it enough for her to be this sexy, ever-available woman?

She groaned. If she knew that he really was innocent, and as honest as the day was long, then she might see a future for them. They were great together, in every way, not only in bed.

The deep lines on her forehead cleared. She would go and talk to her grandfather. Get the exact story. Then she might be able to judge for herself.

Thoughtfully she rose and went to the window for some air. Below in the garden she saw Camilla and Joe, wrapped blissfully in a tender embrace, just staring into one another's eyes.

She winced to see such love. And felt a deep spasm of bitter envy.

CHAPTER TEN

'HURRY!' Vido snapped, wishing he'd taken the wheel.

'No point in taking risks. If we have an accident,' Camilla said soberly, 'you'll be no use to Anna.'

He fumed. Wanted to rant and rave. But knew she was right. 'She's still upset, you say.'

'I've told you everything on the phone, Vido.'

His chest was tight and hurting. Anxiety levels right up with the clouds. 'Tell me again.'

She humoured him—and told him something new. 'Shortly after you left she went to see her grandfather. When she came back she was crying because he'd become agitated and very upset when she'd questioned him about something important to her. He'd mumbled something she didn't understand and patted her hand but she couldn't make any sense of what he'd said.'

Vido's hopes lifted a little. If Anna had tried to get her grandfather to explain what had happened, then she was beginning to question the facts at last.

'And then.'

'The next day, before she could visit the home, the hospital called to say he'd been taken there with a second stroke. When Anna arrived, he managed to smile at her as though his mind was at peace. Then he went to sleep, holding her hand. And passed away without waking up. The doctors said it was inevitable and a merciful release. He was a very sick man.'

Poor Anna. Compassion wrenched at him. 'And...' He checked his watch, fretting. 'The funeral's started!'

'Yes.' She was concentrating hard on the road. 'Vido, haven't you spoken to Anna at all?'

'Every time I called, she burst into tears. Step on it. I want to be there with her.'

'Alive,' Camilla muttered grimly.

Vido barely heard. He was thinking of Anna, forlorn and miserable, devastated by her grandfather's death. He wanted to make everything all right for her. To take away the hurt and unhappiness. The fact that he couldn't achieve any of that was doubly painful for him.

His dark eyes stared sightlessly at the passing countryside. Never in his life had he felt so helpless, so torn by his own futile impotence at making the world a happier place for someone he loved. Not since his mother's breakdown. And this equalled that. He lowered his head and covered his face with his hands as the truth hammered into his pounding skull.

He loved Anna.

'We're here.'

Dazed and bemused, he was out of the car before it came to a stop, half falling, stumbling, frantically regaining his balance and looking around for Anna. At the far end of the small churchyard he saw a small group of people and he ran towards them, only slowing out of respect when he came near.

His hand stole into Anna's. She looked up at him, her face ashen, her eyes filled with tears. And she squeezed his hand so hard that it hurt. But his heart hurt more.

Slender and achingly beautiful in a dark suit, she bent to throw a handful of earth on the coffin. Her head bent in silent prayer and he stayed still and sombre beside her, emotions tearing at him. She seemed so frail. Her lower lip trembled and he had to stop himself from picking her up and whisking her away so that he could hold her and comfort her with the protection of his enclosing arms.

He remembered his own grief for his mother, the sense of anger that she'd died and his own raging frustration that she hadn't lived to see his name cleared.

Anna must be going through some of those helpless feelings, wishing that she'd been able to discuss the past with her grandfather.

And now the old man was dead, she'd never know for sure. Whatever happened between them in the future, she'd always have doubts about him. *Dio.* She might even leave at the end of the six months.

He put his arm around her drooping shoulders, overcome by the emotion that rose to suffocate him. All his instincts were clamouring at him to tell her that he loved her, and always had. But he took one look at her wan, distraught face and huge, dark-circled eyes and knew he couldn't do that now.

It wasn't the right time. He wanted her to believe in him and to accept his love—but she was too bruised and fragile at the moment for rational thought. Later, he promised himself. And felt a little better.

Somehow she kept herself together during the gathering in Stanford House afterwards. As cold and as distant as a zombie, she busied herself handing round snacks and numbly accepted the quiet sympathies of her family, friends and colleagues. At last everyone had gone—except Vido.

'Thank you for coming back,' she said in a small, defeated voice.

He cleared his throat. 'I couldn't stay over there, knowing what you were going through.'

She leant against the wall, utterly weary, emotionally drained. 'What about the job in New York?'

'Unimportant, compared to your needs. I'd done enough research to see what was wrong. I hurled a string of curt and telling directives at them and dumped my report on the chairman's desk. Anna.' His hand touched her shoulder in a gesture of gentle concern. 'You look all in.'

'I've got a terrible headache,' she confessed.

'Go to bed and I'll bring up some hot milk.'

The tenderness in his voice almost made her lose control. Slowly she hauled herself up the stairs, to be overtaken halfway by Vido, who muttered something under his breath, then put down the glass of milk on one of the steps before carrying her to his bed.

Where she lay fully dressed, incapable of doing anything. Gently he removed her clothes from her limp body and sternly ordered her to drink the milk he'd retrieved.

Then he pulled back the sheets and tucked her in. 'Sleep. I'll stay here with you,' he said softly.

Stroking her forehead, he watched her for a long time as she stared blankly into space. His heart ached for her. She'd taken this badly. It amazed him that she'd felt so deeply about her grandfather, who'd never shown her any love. Yet she was loyal, and he had been her only living relative.

At last she slept. Slipping away, he showered and hastily towelled himself dry before crawling back into bed with her. She stirred in her sleep and murmured his name.

'It's all right. I'm here,' he murmured lovingly and took her in his arms.

'Vido!'

Still in the haze of sleep, she reached out for his face and brought her lips to his. There was a desperation in her kiss that touched him profoundly.

'Sweetheart.' And in the anonymity of the night, while she was too drowsy to know what he was saying, he let the words of love rush out softly and fervently. *'Mia cara. Amore mio, mi alma, mi vida, amanda mia...'*

His voice broke. He touched her stomach, wondering if their child had begun to take form there. With all his heart he hoped it had. Silently he vowed that he would care for Anna and cherish her and do everything in his power to clear up the doubts that lay like dark pits between them.

'Please.' A pitiful, miserable mumble.

In the darkness, his control cracking, he put his hand to her face and felt the tears washing down in torrents even though he could tell she was still not fully awake.

'Anna, Anna!'

Fiercely she kissed him, her hands clawing at his arms in a desperate frenzy.

'Make love to me!' she slurred piteously.

'Gently,' he said, his throat thick with emotion.

'No!' She seemed to wake. He could see the whites of her eyes as she gripped him with all her strength. 'Please!'

He held her. Whispered soothingly in her ear. And as he did, he thought of the day when he'd plotted vengeance against her, when he'd felt such scouring lust that he'd wanted her to beg for him. But those feelings had gone. It was breaking his heart to see her so distressed.

'Hush. Sleep,' he breathed, lightly kissing her forehead.

And slowly she subsided. Her sobs that had brought tears to his own eyes grew less frequent and her muscles relaxed. Once or twice she gave a painful, juddering intake of breath, but otherwise she lay quietly in his arms and eventually fell asleep again.

She woke late in the morning. Vido lay beside her, his hair sticking up at odd angles as if he'd had a disturbed night. Careful not to wake him, she wriggled from his embrace and showered away the ravages of her tears from her face.

Darling Vido. He'd flown back from America to be with her. He must be shattered. Musing on his tenderness towards her, she dressed and padded down the stairs to prepare breakfast for him, collecting the post on the way.

While the coffee machine hissed away, she sifted through the mail, putting aside the letters for Vido. Only one was for her and when she saw the writing she froze.

'Grandpa!'

She clutched at the table as the room whirled around. After a moment she felt able to focus again. She checked the envelope. It had been posted—presumably by a nurse—on the day she'd begged her grandfather to tell her just what had happened between him and Vido.

Hastily sitting down, she tore at the flap with shaking fingers, her hand going to her mouth in horror as she read the spidery, almost illegible writing.

It was a confession. He was begging her forgiveness. Saying that he knew he was dying and had to get this off his chest.

She reread the first few sentences, barely able to comprehend what her grandfather was saying. Gradually it became all too clear. The letter fell from her lifeless fingers, unheeded, to the floor.

Her grandfather had lied to her. Far from seeing her as a meal ticket and taking her grandfather's bribe, it seemed that Vido had really cared for her. Only when her grandfather had claimed that she—*she!*—had planted the money in his locker as an act of pure spite, had Vido exploded and wished that she and her grandfather might rot in hell. But her grandfather admitted that it had been he who'd put the money in Vido's locker to blacken him in her eyes.

'Oh, Vido!' she whispered, appalled.

She could almost see them together; her cold-eyed grandfather, the proud Vido reeling from the shock of her supposed treachery.

Typically, she thought, with a little wrench of her heart, he had rejected the bribe. But now she knew why he had eventually taken it. For his mother's sake he had swallowed that great pride of his so that the ailing Sophia could go to Italy to be with her family. Presumably, Anna mused painfully, there had been nothing to keep him in England any longer.

'How could you?' she thought fiercely, aghast at what her grandfather had done. It was worse than she could ever have imagined.

Vido had believed that she was spiteful enough to have deliberately implicated him in the theft.

Suddenly she sat bolt upright, waves of horror crashing through her. No wonder he'd been so hostile when they'd met! He'd behaved as if he had some rather nasty plans for her. Plans…

She swallowed. Had he wanted revenge? Was that why he'd taken her on as his chef? Why he'd seduced her?

She wrestled with this, conceding that he'd been tender and loving, too. There was also the inescapable fact that she loved him. Could she really feel so strongly about a man who was hell bent on deliberately hurting her? Possibly. Her instincts had been wrong about Peter, after all.

Her head ached. She needed to think without interruptions. To be alone for a little while so she could make sense of all this.

Leaving the breakfast half-made, she hurried to her flat and threw a few essential items into a small case. Picking up her handbag, she scrawled a quick note saying that she hoped Vido would understand that she wanted time to herself.

'Please leave me alone,' she wrote. 'I have things to think through. Respect my need.'

Trembling, she placed the note on the kitchen table. Then she hurried out.

Tears blinded her eyes. He'd thought she'd been a bitch. That she'd deliberately shamed him and ruined his name—and his honour that was so precious to him. She didn't know what to think.

Only that she loved him and that he had been very loving towards her. It couldn't be an act—or could it? The questions nagged at her, making her head spin.

Arriving at the cottage, she opened the door and thrust her case into the hall then turned around and began to walk.

She trudged for hours along the narrow lanes, stumbling along, desperately ashamed of what her grandfather had done, weeping for all those angry years when she'd believed that Vido had been brutal and callous.

Her eyes had been opened these past few weeks. He cared about people. She was sure he cared about her, too.

One thing she'd learnt from watching Vido at work. You could never run away from your problems. They stayed with you. Never left your head. You had to tackle them head-on and find a way to solve them.

That was it. A burden seemed to lift from her shoulders. She'd go back to her cottage and ask him to come and talk to her. They wouldn't hold anything back; the resentments, the anger...and whatever feelings they had now. She would tell him how much she loved him and take the risk that he'd laugh in her face.

He might confess that he had wanted vengeance, and that making her fall in love with him was what he'd wanted, so that she'd be hurt when he dumped her. She squared her shoulders. If so, at least she'd know where she stood—

It was then that her thoughts were abruptly cut off when something hit her with an almighty force, spinning her round and dragging her, screaming, along the ground. Dazed and confused, blinded by smoke and choking on acrid fumes, she felt a searing pain leap across her face.

And then everything began to blur till it felt as if she were swimming weightlessly into the depths of a dark blackness as hot as hell.

CHAPTER ELEVEN

SOMEONE was talking. It was a soft Irish voice. A woman. In a fog, Anna listened, her eyelids too heavy to lift.

'Poor girl. That dreadful scar's ruined her looks. It'll never fade. She'll be appalled when she comes to.'

Anna felt pity for the scarred girl wash through her fuddled brain. And after a moment she managed to open her eyes. A nurse was checking her pulse. She frowned and painfully muttered, 'What…?'

'Oh, you're awake!' the Irish voice said, pleased. 'Hello, Anna. You've been in an accident,' she explained. Seeing Anna's frown and wince of pain, she hurried on. 'A joyrider lost control of his car and it hit you then burst into flames. He ran away and a passing motorist found you later—'

'*No!*' She winced with pain but her mind was on the voice that had woken her, and the words of sympathy that had been spoken.

A dreadful scar that would never fade.

Her hand went to her face, which was swathed in bandages. She knew then that the nurse had been talking about her.

'I want a mirror!' she whispered and although the nurse tried to soothe her she kept insisting until one was brought.

'What's it like under there?' she croaked.

'Sure, it's a bit raw now—'

Impatiently she quizzed the consultant who'd come hurrying up. She needed to know the cold, unvarnished truth. Time would tell, apparently. They could do miracles with plastic surgery, he said cheerfully. But in his eyes she could see profound pity. Reading between the lines, she knew that the nurse was probably right.

'Any relative we can contact for you?' the consultant asked. 'Friend?'

'No. Nobody.'

She felt suddenly afraid. If the burns had badly disfigured her, then she would walk out of Vido's life. He had been attracted to her because he thought she was beautiful. But if she was disfigured then he wouldn't want to make love to her again. Her mouth tightened. The last thing she wanted was for him to stay with her out of misguided pity.

*   *   *

Months had passed since he'd last seen Anna. Dispiritedly he trudged into the pub. It was crowded even though it was a weekday lunchtime in October. A sign of good food. His heart leapt—but it had done so many times and he'd had to face disappointment over and over again.

Tense and sick with nerves, he eased through the crowd and nudged himself a place at the bar. It wasn't much as pubs went; one of many sixteenth-century staging posts that littered the Warwickshire countryside around Stratford. But it had suddenly acquired a reputation for home cooking. And Italian dishes. His hands shook and he pressed them hard into the bar counter.

'Guinness, please,' he ordered croakily. 'And a menu.'

'On the blackboard, sir,' the harassed barmaid said with a smile.

He looked around for it, his heart thumping. 'Please let this be the place,' he muttered under his breath.

A blackboard menu meant that dishes were changed frequently, depending on fresh produce available. Promising. He gulped, hardly daring to look.

As he threaded his way through the throng, he imagined he could smell some of his favourites. But he could be deluding himself. He'd been looking for Anna for months and in almost every eating house he'd visited he'd thought *this is the one.*

Her cottage had been sold. The estate agent had refused to give her forwarding address. Why she'd gone, he didn't know, except that she'd been distraught about her grandfather's death. And of course there had been that letter.

He thought of the old man's confession that he'd found discarded on the floor and wished again that he'd been there when she'd read it so that he could have comforted her. She must have been hurt beyond belief to discover that her grandfather had lied so blatantly, and implicated her.

For his part, he had been overwhelmed with relief to discover that she'd had no part in planting the money. And he cursed the old man soundly for ruining their lives.

Initially he'd respected her wish to be alone. But the days had turned to weeks and he'd begun to worry. Ignoring her plea for solitude and missing her badly, he'd felt compelled to search for her.

The blackboard loomed in front of him. He was shaking. He put down his glass on a nearby table before it slopped all over his clothes—clothes that fitted loosely now he'd lost so much weight. But he didn't care about his appearance any more.

His stomach churned as he lifted his gaze and scanned the first item. Nothing special. Nor the next. A feeling of intense misery swelled inside him because he had really hoped...

He froze. *Minestrone alla toscana. Spaghetti al sugo. Spezzatino.* Swaying, he clutched at the table, tears in his eyes. It must be.

Dazed, he hurried to the bar and put in an order. Just the chestnut cake. Waited, his nerves at screaming pitch. Took one mouthful and knew.

On shaky legs, he went outside to sit under the canopy of a huge oak tree. He watched people come and go. Sat there, trembling, waiting, till it was late. And at last she came out of a side door, dressed in a bulky coat, her hair hiding her face as she trudged along the lane to the left of the pub with her head down.

Life powered into him, and he covered the distance between them in swift seconds.

'Anna!' he breathed, inches behind her, his heart thumping fit to burst.

She gasped but didn't turn around. For a moment she froze. 'Go away!' she cried, almost hysterical. And then she hurried on in an odd half-run, half-lope.

So she didn't want to see him. But he had to know why. Since she wasn't running properly, he easily caught her up and put his hands on her shoulders to stop her.

Immediately she wrenched away. 'Leave me alone!' she wailed.

He tried to turn her around but she kept twisting free, almost desperate in her panic.

'What is it?' he asked, perplexed. 'Anna, you must talk to me.' He tried again to make her face him but she screeched at him and his hands fell away.

'No! Go away!' she yelled.

But then he tried again and succeeded finally in turning her to him. Grimly he held on to her arms, determined not to let her go. Her head hung low so that he couldn't see her face. Hurting, aching, he stared at the top of her head in bewilderment.

'I just want to know you're all right. Why you haven't come back—'

'Go,' she muttered. 'It's over. Nothing more to be said.'

'I won't accept that,' he said quietly.

'You must.'

'No, I disagree. You owe me an explanation. I want to know what I've done wrong—'

'Nothing,' she whispered. 'It's not you. Let me go.'

'Where to?' he demanded.

'I have rented a room. Somewhere.'

His confused mind came up with reasons for her disappearance. She didn't love him. That was it. She'd had enough. The death of her grandfather had given her an excuse to leave. She had another lover...

'Anna!' he cried in anguish. 'I'll never rest till you tell me. I have a right to know why you left!'

'To think!'

'Sure. I understand. I read your grandfather's letter. But why stay away?'

She shuddered. 'Why?' she whispered in a terrible, cracked voice. 'You'd better see.'

Her head whipped up. The hair fell back like curtains parting. And he gasped with shock, the horror widening his eyes when he saw the raw skin and the unmistakable scars of a dreadful burn on one side of her face. He stared, paralysed, not even breathing.

'Now you know why it's over. I'm ugly. Undesirable. Again,' she muttered bitterly and pulled away, hurrying on in that odd little loping run.

She'd been right to keep away from him. Vido couldn't be blamed. No one would want to look at someone who was disfigured.

'*Anna!*'

She cried out as she was virtually whirled around, almost losing her balance. Terrified she'd fall, she clutched at him and found herself imprisoned as his hands clamped on her arms.

'Why won't you go?' she moaned. 'You're disgusted by me. I saw you look at me like that all those years ago. You winced then as you winced now. I knew...' She stopped, incapable of continuing.

Once she had believed that he had wanted her as a meal ticket. Whereas he'd just thought she was unbearably ugly. She frowned. That didn't make sense. Her grandfather had been convinced that Vido had really loved her...

'Just a minute.' Frowning hard, Vido seemed to be searching his memory. 'You said I winced?'

'When we had our quarrel,' she muttered.

'Oh, yes. I remember that only too well. It was because I was appalled by your low opinion of me. I was hurt. It was like a stab in the heart. You said that you didn't want to see me again.'

'I—I thought you found me hideous!' she croaked.

'No. Because you'd ruined my hopes. I had such plans for us,' he said passionately. 'I loved you. And you were so cold and cruel. I couldn't believe some of the things you were saying. That's why I flinched.'

'I was hurting,' she explained shakily. 'I pretended I didn't care about what you'd done—what I *thought* you'd done—because I needed to keep a tiny shred of pride if I wasn't to break apart. I had to show I didn't give a damn. But I did,' she confessed, wanting to get everything off her chest. 'I adored you. That's why it had pained me so much to hear those awful things everyone was saying about you and all those women.'

His brows met in a hard golden line. 'They weren't true.'

'I know,' she breathed. 'None of it was. But you can't deny that you find me ugly now.'

'Can't I? I can see beyond that.' He reached out to touch her face but she pulled back, her eyes disbelieving. 'Anna, it was a normal re-action for me to draw back in shock when I saw your poor face. Of course I would. I felt pain for you. I hate to see you hurt. I want to wrap you up in cotton wool and tuck you away so you're never harmed again,' he said with a smile.

'Why?' she asked, blinking in confusion.

'Obvious.' He tilted up her chin and kissed her mouth. 'Because I love you.'

She winced. 'You can't—'

'Don't you tell me what I can and can't do!' he said in amusement.

She glared. 'I don't want your pity!'

'You're not getting it. Your face will heal in time. Even if it didn't, I wouldn't care. Anna, you've got to take pity on me.'

Her eyes widened and she gazed at him in bewilderment. 'On *you*?'

'Yes,' he said, his face unbearably tender. 'I have searched everywhere for you. Every restaurant and café and hotel for miles around. I've eaten meals in dire places, hoping to identify your cooking. And then, today…' He broke off, his voice choking. A thin film of moisture softened the darkness of his eyes. 'Today I tasted your chestnut cake and I knew I'd found you.' His arms came around her. 'You have no idea how happy I felt. And, you know what, Anna?' he murmured.

She was mesmerised by his gaze. 'No. What?' she whispered.

'I was so crazy with excitement I didn't know what to do with myself. I sat outside, waiting for you to finish work. Every time someone emerged from the pub my spirits rose and my heartbeat shot up so far that I'm surprised I'm not on a stretcher on my way to Intensive Care. So take pity on me. Come back.'

Her eyes were huge grey pools. 'I can't!'

'I don't see why.' He touched her face gently. 'First, tell me what happened, *mia adorata*?'

She trembled, weakening. 'It was an accident. A joyrider. I was walking along a country lane, thinking. They believe the driver lost control of the car and it hit me then burst into

flames. He must have run away. A passing motorist found me.'

'But why didn't you contact me?'

'Isn't that obvious?'

'Because you think you're ugly?' he re-
proached.

'I don't *think*. I *am*. I didn't want you to
remember me like this. Or to feel you had to
be nice to me. So I told them at the hospital
that I had no relatives. No friends. I instructed
an agent to sell the cottage and when I came
out of hospital I planned to use the money for
private treatment.'

His fingers lightly touched the livid scar.
'Does it hurt?' he asked with gentle concern.

'Sometimes it itches.'

'I love you.'

'No. You're being noble now.'

There was no mileage in this. She turned her
head away but he forced her to look at him.

'Anna, this isn't some spur-of-the-moment
madness. Or even pity. I loved you when we
were teenagers.' He sighed. 'I know I was only
eighteen, but I had hoped to gain your trust
and ask you to marry me when I was able to
look after you.'

'But...my nose—' she quavered.

'I said. I loved *you*. The woman. The complicated, funny, tender, sensitive, sweet person that you are. As I have come to love you now. Just think of the things that drove us apart. Like…the harem I was keeping, my eagerness to marry an heiress, your wild accusations and your malice in making me out to be a thief. None of those things are true. We both realise that now. You know we were meant for one another, right from the beginning.'

Her eyes closed. 'Oh, dear heaven!' she whispered. She looked at him, her eyes frantic, and she staggered a little. 'I—I need to sit down—'

'Come with me.'

He put his arm around her shaking shoulders, noticing how frail she was and how defensive. She was hugging her coat about her as if she wanted to stay isolated and alone. But he wouldn't allow that.

'Where are we going?' she asked weakly as they reached the car.

'Home. Stanford House.'

She was silent, her fingers twisting in her lap nervously. He pushed in a CD and the soothing sound of Mozart filled the car.

'You're very thin,' she said in a small voice.

'Worry.' He pushed his hand through his hair. 'I've been out of my mind. And when I found your grandfather's letter and I knew that you'd had no part in the accusation of theft against me, I felt a huge sense of guilt that I'd ever believed the evil old man.'

'He always liked to get his own way,' she mumbled. 'And I think he knew he'd met his match in you because you stood up to him.'

'But why was he unkind to you?' he probed angrily.

'Poor Grandpa,' she mused. 'He loved my father very much. I think he half blamed me for father's death. My parents had gone away on holiday, you see. I was just ten months old. But they missed me dreadfully and Father drove from Scotland right through the night. Tiredness made him misjudge a corner and he and Mother were killed outright. Grandpa couldn't look at me without seeing my father's broken body on the mortuary slab. I know it was unfair of him to dislike me but all his hopes and dreams had been smashed to smithereens by that car crash. He'd looked forward to my father taking over the factory after him and often told me that.'

'Tactless old man!' Vido muttered.

'Yes. But he couldn't help himself. He was wrapped up in his misery. I don't think he ever recovered from his grief and he was a very bitter and unhappy man. I felt sorry for him and wished I could have taken my father's place.'

'You're very generous in accepting his treatment of you,' Vido muttered.

She gave a faint smile. 'I understand how love and passion can distort things. They make you irrational. It's like being on drugs.'

Vido's mouth compressed and he didn't comment. She leaned her head back, feeling utterly wiped out. When they arrived at the house, he took her into the drawing room, sat her down and brought her a brandy.

'No, thanks.'

Looking tousled and distracted, he drank it. And she drank him in, loving the familiar face, anxious at how sharp his cheekbones had become. He said he loved her. Could that really be true? The very thought made her dizzy.

'I think,' he said, sitting on the sofa beside her and taking her hands in his, 'you were ready to believe those bad things about me because all your life you'd been told you were ugly. Your self-esteem was too low for you to believe that I liked you, let alone might care deeply about you.'

'I'm so sorry,' she said fervently. 'But everything I was told seemed to make perfect sense. You were popular and devastatingly handsome. It was beyond belief that you should like me. The only explanation was that you must be after my money. Everyone thought that.'

'I understand. But you and they were wrong.' He lifted her hand and kissed her fingers with heartbreaking tenderness. 'Let me take your coat—'

'No!' In panic she clutched the hideous thing more tightly to her. 'Just...tell me that you love me. Really, really love me!'

'Darling. I do. I'm insanely in love with you. I think about you all the time—'

'But...my face...'

'Will you listen, woman?' he said in mock exasperation. 'I don't care about your face. I'm only sorry you've had to go through this on your own. However, I'm here now and you won't get rid of me this time.'

'You couldn't...ever *want* me,' she said jerkily.

He kissed her. Sweetly he moved his lips over her face and with the lightest of butterfly kisses he let his mouth touch her disfiguring scars. His breathing quickened. Then he took her hand and placed it on his groin.

'Sez who?' he murmured.

Tears formed in her eyes. 'Vido!' she said brokenly.

'It's not a cause for tears!' he declared, pretending to be indignant.

She laughed and cried at the same time. 'No!' she agreed.

'Marry me,' he urged. 'Be my wife. Wife,' he repeated, as if tasting the word with pleasure. 'My wife!'

Her eyes rounded in astonishment. 'Marry you?' she squeaked.

'Yes. It's a legal process where a man and a woman get dressed up in ridiculous clothes and spend a fortune on—'

'Vido!' she reproved, laughing.

'That's better. Please. Put me out of my misery. Think of my staff. They've suffered my moody silences and poor performance and grumbles about the temporary chef for too long. Marry me. Today. Tomorrow, whenever, I don't care, just say yes!'

She took a deep breath. Plunged into happiness. 'Yes!' she squeaked.

He kissed her long and slow. His hands drifted over her shoulders. She was absolutely still as he pushed off her concealing coat.

'I love you so much!' he breathed and hazily he stared at her. She was eyeing him in wary apprehension. 'What? What's the matter?'

She could hardly breathe. 'Use your eyes, Vido!'

Her gaze dropped to look at her waist and so did his. He blinked. Looked again. His eyes closed.

'Mia futura mamma!' His eyes snapped open again and happiness lit his face as he took Anna's face between his hands. 'Oh, my darling! A baby! Our baby! You and me... This is something I'd hoped for, longed for—it was a mistake, I know, but when I thought you might be pregnant I—I—sweetheart, I'm rambling. Are you all right? Do you need to lie down or something—?'

'No!' she said, her eyes shining. 'Stop flapping. I'm disgustingly well. You're pleased?'

'Pleased?' He leapt up, strode around the room as if an excess of energy was pushing him along. 'Pleased. Huh! Try ecstatic.

Exhilarated. Intoxicated with joy. It's...
elettrizzaaante.'

Watching his delight, she felt suddenly safe
and serene. 'Oh, Vido,' she breathed. 'I was
so thrilled when I discovered I was pregnant.
I've been cherishing our baby all these weeks.
I—I believed it was all I had of you.'

In the middle of his energetic wandering, he
spun around, his eyes darkening. 'You weren't
going to tell me?' he shot indignantly.

'Don't be angry with me. I couldn't bear the
thought that you might insist on marrying me
because of our child,' she said.

'I would. Of course I would—'

'Exactly. You're an honourable man. But
how do you think I would have felt, never
knowing if you'd proposed because you felt
sorry for my disfigured face—and because I
was pregnant? I couldn't bear that. You might
have hated me for the rest of your life. And I
was afraid that a shotgun marriage to me could
have ruined your chance of happiness with a
woman you'd love.'

'*Dio!*' he whispered, hurrying over and
holding her close. '*You're* the woman I love!
And I almost lost you and our child.'

'But you didn't,' she smiled. 'The chestnut cake saw to that.'

'You will definitely stay?' He gave a shaky grin. 'The kitchen's been done.'

'Oh, that changes everything,' she said with a laugh. 'Show me. I'm dying for a cup of tea.'

'Anything else?' he murmured, pulling her to her feet. 'Rhubarb on toast? Vinegar sandwiches?'

Anna laughed. 'Just tea,' she said with an intensely happy sigh. 'And you and our baby and love.' She kissed him, deliriously happy. 'What more,' she murmured softly, 'could a girl ever want?'

MILLS & BOON® PUBLISH EIGHT LARGE PRINT TITLES A MONTH. THESE ARE THE EIGHT TITLES FOR JANUARY 2005

❦

THE MAGNATE'S MISTRESS
Miranda Lee

THE ITALIAN'S VIRGIN PRINCESS
Jane Porter

A PASSIONATE REVENGE
Sara Wood

THE GREEK'S BLACKMAILED WIFE
Sarah Morgan

HIS HEIRESS WIFE
Margaret Way

THE HUSBAND SWEEPSTAKE
Leigh Michaels

HER SECRET, HIS SON
Barbara Hannay

MARRIAGE MAKE-OVER
Ally Blake

MILLS & BOON®

Live the emotion

1204 Rom LP

MILLS & BOON® PUBLISH EIGHT LARGE PRINT TITLES A MONTH. THESE ARE THE EIGHT TITLES FOR FEBRUARY 2005

———————— ❧ ————————

MISTRESS TO HER HUSBAND
Penny Jordan

THE GREEK TYCOON'S LOVE-CHILD
Jacqueline Baird

THE FORBIDDEN MISTRESS
Anne Mather

THE SICILIAN'S BOUGHT BRIDE
Carol Marinelli

TO CATCH A GROOM
Rebecca Winters

THE BRIDE PRIZE
Susan Fox

HIRED BY MR RIGHT
Nicola Marsh

FOR OUR CHILDREN'S SAKE
Natasha Oakley

MILLS & BOON®

Live the emotion

0105 Rom LP

All the characters in this book have no existence outside
the imagination of the author, and have no relation
whatsoever to anyone bearing the same name or names.
They are not even distantly inspired by any individual
known or unknown to the author, and all the incidents
are pure invention.

All Rights Reserved including the right of reproduction
in whole or in part in any form. This edition is published
by arrangement with Harlequin Enterprises II B.V. The
text of this publication or any part thereof may not be
reproduced or transmitted in any form or by any means,
electronic or mechanical, including photocopying,
recording, storage in an information retrieval system,
or otherwise, without the written permission of
the publisher.

MILLS & BOON and
MILLS & BOON with the Rose Device
are registered trademarks of the publisher.

First published in Great Britain 2004
Large Print edition 2005
Harlequin Mills & Boon Limited,
Eton House, 18-24 Paradise Road,
Richmond, Surrey TW9 1SR

© Sara Wood 2004

ISBN 0 263 18517 6

Set in Times Roman 16½ on 17¾ pt.
16-0105-48677

Printed and bound in Great Britain
by Antony Rowe Ltd, Chippenham, Wiltshire

A PASSIONATE REVENGE

BY

SARA WOOD

MILLS & BOON®

A PASSIONATE
REVENGE

DM